A Bounty on Forever

by

Connie Y Harris

The Forever Series, Book 2

A Bounty on Forever

Cover Art by *Tina Lynn Stout*

The Wild Rose Press, Inc.
PO Box 708
Adams Basin, NY 14410-0708
Visit us at www.thewildrosepress.com

Publishing History
First Crimson Rose Edition, 2019
Print ISBN 978-1-5092-2970-3
Digital ISBN 978-1-5092-2971-0

The Forever Series, Book 2
Published in the United States of America

Wolf whistles and catcalls drowned out Tony's words as he lifted Sierra's dress high on her thigh. She sucked in her breath as his hand skimmed the inside of her leg. Goosebumps popped up along her arms and the pit of her stomach somersaulted. She gazed at the top of his uncovered head, fixated on the thick layers of textured hair while he adjusted the garter a few inches above her knee. With an uncontrollable urge to massage the deep brown mop, she scrunched and poised her fingers an inch from contact but froze when he raised his head and locked eyes with her. *Did he have x-ray vision?* She gasped, dropped her arms, and plopped her hands in her lap.

His eyes, almost black with intensity, messaged clear desire as he offered his hand. "Want to dance?"

Her nipples hardened and moisture dampened her thighs. "Sure," she squeaked.

The notes of a slow song drifted across the dance floor. *No pressure, no pressure, no pressure*. She stepped onto the platform and was hugged into a ripped chest. Engulfed by the musk scent, she laid her head on his shoulder, her nose pressed into his warm neck. The silence screamed while their feet shuffled together across the floor without missing a beat. The song ended too soon. *Aren't there more lyrics?*

As they drew apart, he said, "Thanks." And offered a smoldering look. "Am I forgiven?"

Ay dios mio. I'm a goner.

Dedication

One of the most important jobs in the military
is a parachute rigger,
the person who packs your parachute.
You depend on that individual
for a safe landing every time you jump.
This book is dedicated to the Zumba community
and all the talented instructors
who inspire and uplift me on a daily basis.
They pack my parachute.

Acknowledgments

Special thanks to Yineth Zuniga, my Colombian muse.
To Joel Anderson,
who allowed me a peek inside circus life.
To Abbi Carr
for expert answers to questions about law school.
And to nurses, Mary and Cathy,
who saved my manuscript from the firing line.

Chapter One

Tony Franco, RN, dressed in green hospital scrubs, pushed through the double doors of the busy emergency room at the Southern Cal Medical Center and found himself nose to nose with his former executive officer from SEAL Team Two.

"There's a bounty on your head, Petty Officer."

Garbed in civvies, the ever-present SEAL trident missing from his chest, the Executive Officer's stoic expression gave away nothing, but his voice conveyed the same serious tone he used when issuing orders for a life or death mission.

"Do we need a private place to talk?" Tony asked, nonplussed as he peeled the thin, nitrile gloves off his hands and stuffed one inside the other before tossing them into a nearby trash bin.

Glancing around the sparse area, the sandy-haired man squared his shoulders and nodded. "Why I showed up in the middle of the night."

"Follow me, XO." Tony tilted his head in the direction of the hall and stepped out in front. With a brisk gait, he led the way down a narrow corridor to a gated entrance. He flashed his security badge over the card reader and a metal lock released with a snap. "You realize, I'm not in the Navy anymore." He opened the gate and then stepped back, allowing the senior-ranked man first passage into the secure area.

"Doesn't matter. You'll always be a SEAL." The XO followed Tony into a small space packed with equipment. A large metal cylinder, resembling a small submarine, lay in the middle of the room. "Hyperbaric chamber?" he asked, gazing at the complex set-up of gauges and lights.

"Lots of scuba diving in the Los Angeles area. We treat divers for the bends after they surface too fast."

The XO scoffed. "I'm familiar."

Tony nodded his agreement. "It's why I originally got hired. They needed someone with my expertise on dive procedure."

The bigger man shifted his weight and checked his watch. "Seems like a good gig."

Tony noticed the officer's impatience and released the airtight lever on the outside hull before ducking his head as he stepped through the circular metal threshold. "Best thing is it's sound-proof once I turn off the microphone." He stabbed a button just inside the hatch and flipped the switch to the off position, smiling as he stooped forward to navigate the cramped space. "Complete privacy."

"You haven't lost your well-honed security skills, Franco," the XO quipped as he slipped through the round door and tugged it closed.

"Roger that. So," Tony asked, "who wants my head on a stick?"

He sat on the narrow, blue-painted ledge across from his former commander and propped his elbows on his knees, interested but not too concerned about the revelation someone wanted him offed. Combat does that to a man. Daily threats of being blown up by an IED or having your head chopped off in front of a camera are real backbone builders.

"We received an alert via Naval Intelligence regarding an injured combatant you treated on your last tour in Iraq." He inhaled deeply before continuing. "Nothing quite like the cool tang of extra oxygen."

Tony nodded, then sat up and rubbed his temple. "I remember a twentyish Iraqi male from my last mission. Gunshot wound, held for questioning at a black site."

In a trademark habit, the XO tugged on his right earlobe. "That'd be the one."

"I don't get it. The CIA asked for assistance. My Team and I were in the area. I stabilized him and recommended evac. Why would he be after me?"

"He isn't. His father, Mohammed Ali Aboud, is the bastard who wants you dead."

Remembering the asshole in question, the former SEAL rubbed the back of his neck. "Jesus sir, Ali Aboud isn't just a bastard. He's a prominent ISIS leader as well as a sheik with tons of cash and resources.

"True and he blames you for his son's death."

Tony's brow scrunched into a frown. "Wait a minute. You said *death*. I left the kid alive."

"Apparently, after you headed stateside, the CIA goons conducted an enhanced interrogation on him and opened his wounds." He exaggerated an eye roll. "The spooks let jihadi junior bleed out."

"But there were cameras in the room which would show the interrogation tactics used. Can't the Navy use diplomatic channels to sort this shit sandwich out?"

"The recording of his 'interviews' disappeared. You're the last person logged in who visited his cell and witnessed him alive. Ali Aboud's world view demands an eye for an eye. He posted the bounty on a notorious dark web terrorist blog our intel guys monitor. One of them picked up the threat and reported up the chain of command.

Tony told himself to remain calm while he gathered his own intel. He'd need his own plan of action. "Any idea of their current location, I assume we're talking more than one?"

"Latest reports show Aboud's assassins crossing the border from Mexico. They vanished once they were stateside."

"Vanished?" He slammed the bottom of his fist into the curved wall of the chamber, adrenalin pulsing through his body. "And I'm just now being notified?" The threat was real and the danger potentially close. "What the fuck…. Sir?"

The XO didn't flinch, didn't blink. "How's your family?"

"Why?" Tony countered, knowing full well that he needed to rope in his anger. Uncontrolled emotions at a time like this could cloud his judgment.

"These people are ruthless. If they can't find you, they'll come after anyone you love who could tell them your whereabouts."

"No worries there, for the most part. I'm married to the job and I'm an only child."

"What about your parents? They still living?"

He puffed out a breath of air. "My mother married a truck driver, assumed his last name and moved to a small Northern California town. They're pretty much off the map. My father died from AIDS a few years back." In response to the question mark framing the XO's face, Tony added, "Don't ask."

With a nod, the senior officer retrieved a small

piece of paper from his jacket pocket, along with his U.S. government issue black ball point. With smooth precision, he penned a brief note, then folded it in half and stuffed the small square in Tony's fisted hand. "My number if you need anything. Ramp up your personal security ASAP. These guys aren't going to come in guns blazing. They'll hunt you down and quietly put a bullet in your head or manufacture an accident."

"Will do." *Right after I attend my closest friend's wedding next week.* He unlatched the heavy lever and heaved open the massive steel door. *He's like a brother and I'm not leaving him high and dry, no matter who wants me dead.*

The unmistakable weight of the target on his back contracted Tony's shoulder muscles into tight knots. He forced a stiff, thin-lipped smile and shook hands with his former XO. "Thanks for the head's up, Sir."

"I've assigned all available resources to scour every intelligence channel. We'll locate these guys." He clutched Tony's hand in a reassuring grip. "Watch your ass, Franco."

Squaring his shoulders, the XO disappeared down the hall with the signature swagger of the SEAL Team Two Executive Officer.

****

Although Tony sometimes missed the adrenaline rush of serving on the battlefield as a corpsman, the transition to the civilian world as a nurse practitioner fulfilled one of his most important life goals. He simply liked helping people.

The beep, beep, beep from his hospital tablet jerked his attention as he stepped out of the secure area. With the signal restored, several messages, all marked *urgent*, downloaded. *Holy hell.*

As he mentally prioritized the emergencies, one blazed to the top: young female, presenting with severe headache and nausea.

The khaki colored walls of the long corridor to Emergency Room Two swept by under Tony's gait. Due to the recent rise in the number of young females presenting with acute ischemic attacks in their brains, he didn't break stride as he pivoted around the curtain for what might be a patient with an imminent stroke.

"Hello, Ms. Sanchez." He entered the cubicle and with a quick and, he hoped, inconspicuous glance at her personal info. "Miss Sierra Sanchez, can you tell me the current month and your date of birth?"

"It's April. My birthday is September 9th, 1984."

She's alert and someone hooked her up with an IV. Good. He smiled and continued, "How long have you had this headache?" Acutely aware of slurred speech in stroke victims, he focused on her lips as she swiped her tongue over them before forming a response.

She pinched her brow and sighed. "It started earlier this evening, so I tried to sleep it off, which sometimes works, but the pain wasn't going away."

Perfect pronunciation with a slight foreign accent he couldn't place. He went through the standard stroke assessment before taking her blood pressure. "On a scale of one to ten what is your pain level?"

"I wouldn't have come to the emergency room for less than a seven."

"You did the right thing. Are you allergic to any medications?" he asked, noticing the tight shorts and muscular legs as they stretched over the length of the exam table.

"No."

"Any nausea?

"Yes, Doctor. I vomited my dinner, but it was airplane food, so you know." She started to laugh, then grimaced. "I have a history of migraines, accompanied by nausea. My doctor prescribed generic Sumatriptan which usually works wonders. Unfortunately, I left the medicine at home."

Time to triage this conversation. "I'm a nurse practitioner, not a doctor, but I can order something for the pain and nausea." He popped a thermometer in her mouth and continued. "With your pattern of symptoms and history of migraines, I don't think it's anything more serious, but I can diagnosis you with a good sense of humor considering your pain level."

Her shoulders shook as she attempted to laugh while keeping the thermometer between her lips. *God, she's cute.*

He took her pulse while waiting for the beep from the thermometer. "Ninety-eight-six," he said and discarded it into the hazardous waste bin. "No fever. Ready for those meds?"

Brushing thick dark curls from her face with one hand, she extended the other, open palm. "Bring it on."

Tony stepped a few feet away and typed his exam findings, recommendations and orders for meds into the tablet. On his return to the cubicle, he found Sierra trying to get out of bed. He was just fast enough to catch her as she swayed, hitting him squarely in the chest with flattened palms, putting her close enough to inhale her subtle floral scent. A very enticing scent.

"Easy does it, Miss Sanchez," he said as he guided her to a nearby recliner. "Sit." He gripped her elbow with his free hand as she complied. "The meds I ordered could cause drowsiness. If the pain worsens or doesn't improve with the Sumatriptan, come back here immediately." After reviewing the symptoms of stroke with her, he asked, "Do you have a way home?"

She lifted her chin and flipped her hair behind her shoulder. "I used a ride share service from the hotel. I can ride share back but thanks for the offer."

He chuckled. "Okay."

A nurse appeared at the edge of the curtain, holding a small paper cup. "I'll take it from here," Tony said as he took the cup and checked the contents before stepping to the sink and filling a second cup with water.

Handing Sierra the pill cup, then the water, he said, "Down the hatch."

She tossed the pills in her mouth and swallowed without any difficulty. "Good job. You're familiar with this medication so you know you should feel some relief in a few minutes." Tony grabbed a wheelchair from the corner of the room and rolled it to the side of the recliner.

She peered at the mode of transport with disdain. "I don't need help. I can walk." Using the cushioned arms of the recliner, she thrust herself up, then wobbled and sat back down with a groan and a thud.

Acting on impulse, Tony leaned in until their noses almost touched. Close enough to smell the fresh peppermint of her toothpaste, he peered into her emerald green eyes. "Stay put until the doctor comes in to discharge you. Rest."

Without flinching, she flung her arms around his neck and returned his steady gaze. Paralyzed with indecision, his mind raced. He wanted to kiss her...bad.

Professional ethics prohibited him from making a move on a patient. She searched his face for a few seconds and then, as if she read his mind, closed her eyes and parted her lips. *Oh, hell.*

Debate raged as he fought the desire to tilt his head and start a slow descent toward those full cherry lips and for one brief second, the hectic world of the emergency room and very real death threats fell away.

From the hallway outside, pounding footsteps, accompanied by shouts of, "Inbound gunshot victim," brought reality crashing back.

Tony jerked away from Sierra, yanked the curtain open and yelled for a nurse.

"Gotta go," he said, shrugging as he splayed his hands, hoping she'd see his disappointment. "I want to see you again." After scribbling his phone number on her arm, he began backing out of the room and mouthed, "Call me," then turned and raced toward the commotion.

****

With the echo of rapidly retreating footsteps in the background, Sierra Sanchez glanced at the ink on her arm, then stared at the empty space outside her curtained cocoon. "Wait. What's your name?"

A loud crash interrupted her trance-like fixation on the hotter than anything she'd ever seen on TV nurse who just left her with a pounding heart and a dry mouth. An older man, fifty-something, stumbled into the metal cart left at the end of her bed as he focused on his tablet.

His head jerked up. "Oh, didn't see that." He half-smiled, as a bright shade of red spread across his face. "I was reviewing the nurse's notes on your treatment and agree with his recommendations." He stuck out his hand. "Dr. Stein."

"Sierra Sanchez," she said, all the while debating if she should ask Stein for the nurse's name. No way, she decided. *I'll bet every female patient he treats wants his name. Best to give it a week or two and then call him.*

"Says here, you have a history of migraines," Dr. Stein murmured. "And that you have a prescription for them but forgot to bring the medication on your trip? Is that correct?"

"Yes. I have a prescription for Sumatriptan, ten milligrams."

"Per the nurse's notes, he recommends something for nausea as well. I'll give you a script for the appropriate meds for nausea and pain, enough to last you until you get home, then I'll release you." He gazed at the wheelchair. "Do you need assistance out?"

Why doesn't he say the nurse's name? "No. I can walk." *Go ahead. Say his name, doc.* And thanks for the prescriptions, doctor." *Maybe a leading question or comment?* "Oh, so you know, the nurse, I didn't catch his name, was exceptional."

"Oh, we're lucky to have him with us."

A young female with a name tag that said LPN Stansfield, entered the room and after a nod to the doctor and a reassuring smile for Sierra, removed the IV from her arm before applying a cotton ball topped with tape. As quickly as she appeared, she disappeared into the long, monochrome corridor.

Without warning, *Code blue, code blue, ER room four. Code blue, code blue, ER room four. . .* burst from the public address system.

The doctor turned and streaked out of the room,

white coat flapping behind his skinny legs. "See the cashier on your way out."

Sierra lifted herself out of the recliner muttering about bad timing. She followed the signs for the exit and found the cashier. Tempted as she was to march back in the hospital, locate the nurse and write her phone number on his arm, with a statement of, "there," she opted for a cab. The lack of sleep from last night started to envelope her and a hot shower called to her more than a hot nurse.

Chapter Two

The U.S. Navy SEALS arrived at Wildwood Farms commando style under their tartan kilts. But damn, Tony would go butt naked to see his best friend and former Echo Platoon mate, Gavin Cross, wrapped in the kind of happiness the day's events would bring.

Bottom line, Gavin deserved a happy ending, or beginning, depending how you viewed life. After the emotional roller coaster which followed Operation Firestorm and his uphill battle recovering from a traumatic brain injury, Gavin had faced his biggest challenge capturing the heart of his soon to be wife, Ariel Armstrong. But one thing was certain, no matter the odds, his buddy would conquer any obstacle put in front of him with stubborn will and win.

Today, his friend had won the life lottery.

Tony Franco delved into the leather sporran hanging around his waist and slid out the Trident he'd stowed there. He pinned the insignia on his plaid cloth-covered chest completing his 'best man at the wedding' outfit. With such a large contingent of special operators descending on the quaint farm town of Ocala, Florida, he believed it prudent to arrive incognito rather than advertise the fact he was one of them. In Los Angeles, where he'd lived and worked since his enlistment ended, you could wear a clown costume in a restaurant, and no one blinked an eye. But here in a rural southern community, there were plenty of yahoos itching for bragging rights that they'd bested a Navy SEAL in a fistfight. He smiled at the thought. And then there was the trivial matter of the bounty on his head.

"Tony, my God, you're here," Gavin shouted across the gravel driveway. "Right on time for lunch." His contagious smile stretched across a mouthful of perfect, white teeth.

"Yeah, bro," Tony shouted back. "I wouldn't miss the opportunity to see the Caveman become civilized," he said, referring to Gavin's nickname while on the SEAL Teams.

"Very funny, since you're the son of a bitch responsible for giving me that reputation." After a fist bump, the two men hugged hard enough to lift Tony in a slight bounce off the ground. His mind stuttered for the words that wouldn't ruin the day for his best friend but also let him know he cared. "Hey man, I was sorry to hear about your dad."

Gavin's demeanor switched from relaxed and happy to serious and somber. "His heart." He cleared his throat. "His heart gave out." He swallowed so hard his Adam's apple floated up and down in his throat. "I just wish he could have been here today."

"He is, bro." Tony patted Gavin on the shoulder and pointed skyward. "He's got a bird's eye view."

"Yeah. Watching me do hard labor on this farm." Gav's smile widened. "Between you and me, I do love living here and having Ariel with me, well, it makes each day a gift."

"I get it, man, but something's missing."

"What?"

"The frown lines and infamous death stare."

"Asshole."

"Seriously, I can tell farm life agrees with you." *Especially after a Taliban sniper almost snuffed out your lights.*

Gavin nodded toward the stunning woman standing, hands clasped over her heart, in the doorway of the family's palatial farmhouse. "She's the other reason I'm alive."

Aware of his friend's enforced R&R from active duty, thanks to his reluctant report up his command channels, Tony ignored the comment and the sudden squeeze in his chest from the reminder. To lighten the mood, he glanced in the woman's direction. "I take it the hot babe is also the bride?"

"Her name is Ariel, numb-nuts," Gavin said. "But you already know that." His face brightened. "She is a total class act." He waved her over. "What about you? Found a soft place to land yet?"

An image of Sierra Sanchez popped into Tony's head and he almost nodded yes. But after a week of anticipation, there'd been no phone call from the stunning beauty. Instead, he shook his head, "Nah. Not in my immediate future." *If I even have a future.*

"Yeah," Gavin scoffed. "Career comes first."

Tony nodded his head. "I finished my advanced nursing degree. California is one of those states that gives credit for experience as a Navy corpsman, so the degree path was a short runway and I'm official now. It's the perfect gig."

"You know what they say about all work and no play, my friend."

"Says the most serious guy in history." Tony scoffed. "I'm not saying there haven't been some temptations." His mind again flashed an image of dark curly hair and cherry lips. "But you guys, The Team guys, are my family. Why I'm here." *Despite the fact someone is trying to kill me.*

His gaze followed Gavin's as Ariel picked her way across the paving stones in spiked heels, which matched her nude-colored, knitted maxi dress. Tony concluded Gavin hit the jack pot. He'd seen a picture, but it didn't do her justice. The clingy fabric hugged her subtle curves and accentuated her firm, just-right breasts. With thumb and forefinger, she lifted her dress and revealed a glimpse of long, defined, suntanned legs. He observed the eye contact between bride and groom and a surge of envy jolted him. She's the real deal. Gavin found his soul mate.

Ariel, her hand outstretched, offered a warm smile accompanied by the wafting scent of blooming honeysuckle. Tony breathed in the aroma of the subtle sweetness and clasped the soft skin with a firm grip. "Nice to finally meet you, Ariel.

"Likewise, Tony." She winked. "I've heard so much about you."

"Uh, oh. Don't believe anything he said about me. They're all lies."

"Oh, I see." She gave Tony a wry grin, "So, you're not the best corpsman in the history of the Navy?"

Oh, she's a handful and perfect for Gavin, he thought to himself. "Well, that part's true."

"How was the red-eye from LA?" Ariel asked.

"Uneventful." He stuck his hands in his pants pockets. "Which in my world…a welcomed relief."

"Did they feed you on the plane?" Gavin chimed in. "Are you hungry?"

"I ate but I wouldn't call it food." Tony mimed sticking his finger down his throat. "I could definitely snack on something light and maybe drink a beer."

"You got it. Come with me." Ariel tucked her arm through his and tugged him toward a picnic table covered with a checkered cloth and a buffet of farm fresh vegetables, smoked bar-b-que and grilled chicken.

Tony surveyed his options while taking in a whiffs the appealing hickory smell and smacked his lips. "This is quite a spread."

Ariel smiled in response. "Feel free to grab a bite before the dress rehearsal. Afterward, we'll officially chow down." She handed him a dinner plate as she called over her shoulder to Gavin, "Babe, grab your buddy something ice cold to drink."

Tony observed his former team leader do as he was asked and redeploy toward a large aluminum container full of ice and drinks. "Thanks Ariel. I appreciate your hospitality, but I can wait to eat after the rehearsal." He smoothed his hand over the rectangular piece of wool cloth draped over his left shoulder. "Besides, I don't want to spill sauce on my tartan."

Ariel arched one brow. "You're acting like you're a guest but after what you did for Gavin in Afghanistan, you are family to me."

Tony swallowed hard, moved by her unconditional acceptance of him. "Beer sounds great because dress rehearsals in kilts with a bunch of crazy SEALS always go better with beer."

Gavin handed him a brown glass bottle. Pressed to his lips, Tony consumed several steady gulps before tossing the empty into a nearby metal trash can. "Ahhh, nectar of the Gods."

Ariel shook her head with a laugh, whipping waves of light brown hair over her shoulders and said, "We have napkins or hand towels or sheets." She continued with a chuckle, "But if you'd prefer, I can have the housekeeper make you a quick ham sandwich."

"Would that housekeeper go by the name, Bessie Mae?"

"The one and only. I take it you've visited Gavin here and understand the rules of engagement with her?"

"Oh yes." Tony ignored the sound of Gavin's fake choking but understood the translation and signaled 'thumbs up' behind his back.

His lips were sealed about the antics they'd committed as young Naval recruits who spent their leave on the Cross farm, especially the one involving strippers, and a keg. But under Bessie Mae's watchful eye, they got caught…skinny dipping. The horrified indignity on her face, when she ordered them all out of the water, still made him laugh. He mimicked the spinster, bun wound in a tight knot on her head, her furrowed uni-brow, shaking an index finger. He left off the part where she called the girls harlots before she shooed them away.

Ariel hugged his arm tighter and chuckled. "Your imitation's dead-on and funny but we're too smart to share it with her, right?" They changed course for the house and zigzagged up the sloped stairs toward the screened kitchen door.

"Listen, Tony." Her face smoothed into an earnest mien. "It was my request to wear wedding attire for the rehearsal so don't hold it against Gavin. I wanted to ensure we had time to do any needed alterations, and with you guys arriving from all over the world…well, tomorrow would be too late.

Tony glanced back and caught Gavin's smug expression, like a miner who just discovered gold in the Klondike. "No big deal. We like the chance to wear something other than cargo pants and leather sandals."

Wait until the happy bastard discovers what his teammates have cooked up for him tonight after the festivities.

****

Sierra Sanchez peered out the second story window of the cottage where her best friend since high school now lived and worked as the farm vet for one of the wealthiest families in Marion County, Florida. She followed the evaporating trail of dust marking the SEAL exodus as they barreled down the rocky drive toward the exit. "I'm so sorry I missed the rehearsal and the dinner, Ariel."

"You couldn't help your flight got canceled. Besides, you'd be late to your own wedding." Ariel cupped her palm against her lips to stifle a giggle. "And, without a doubt, your own funeral."

"Okay, okay, I'm famous for being tardy but attending the Zumba Master Class in Los Angeles this close to your wedding was a mistake." Sierra paused for a second. "Except for the hot emergency room nurse who was no mistake." She waggled her eyebrows. "I still should have canceled."

"Uh, you were billed as the star presenter, and the only thing you missed…wait a minute—" Planting both fists on her hips, Ariel demanded, "Why would you need a hot nurse in an emergency room?"

Sierra snorted the mouth full of wine. "I'm okay. You know those migraines I get?" She didn't wait for a response. "A nasty one hit me in the middle of the night. I forgot my meds and couldn't sleep so I got myself to the closest hospital emergency room. The on-call nurse who treated me was…. well, dreamy."

Ariel made a rolling motion with one hand, "And…?"

"And, he wrote his phone number on my arm and told me to call him."

"Does said 'hot nurse' have a name? And have you called him?"

"Promise not to laugh, but I was so buzzed from the meds he gave me, I floated back to the hotel, took a shower and washed off the ink." She heaved a deep sigh and splayed her hands outward "…. oops."

"You could always call the hospital and ask for him by name."

Sierra winced. "Uh, like I said, the pain was off the charts and I'm not sure he even had a name tag, maybe a badge around his neck but I couldn't read the print."

"In other words, you got nothing?"

"Nothing, nada, zilch."

"Oh boy. Well, this might make you feel better. The one thing you missed by being late was a practice march down the aisle with Gavin's best man, a stone-cold double take, maybe even a triple take."

"Oh, you don't say." She batted her eyelashes and pictured the LA nurse as her version of a double take. "Well, speaking of Gavin's best man, I spotted a group of guys in kilts pile into an SUV and tear out of here like they were headed for free beer. I assume he was one of them?"

"Close and yes. Happy hour at the nearest country bar, Eight Seconds in Gainesville, but after they change clothes…in the car." She laughed. "I hope. Cause there's no back-up if their kilts get drunk-destroyed."

"Did those guys have anything on under the kilts?"

"Leave it to you, my inquisitive friend, to want that tidbit of information."

"Well?" Sierra asked.

"Tradition dictates they go commando."

"One can always hope tomorrow is windy."

With a devilish grin, Ariel completed Sierra's thought. "The idea of six battle-hardened alpha males dressed in kilts on a breezy day is quite a visual." Eyebrows raised and eyes wide she added, "Time to check the weather while we wait for the other bridesmaids to change into comfy clothes. The earlier report said sunny and warm so a gust or two of wind could be a welcomed relief from the ever-present Florida humidity."

Hands raised in a child-like clap, Sierra raced ahead of Ariel to the computer desk and plopped down on the swivel chair, sending the seat and her twirling in a full circle. She tapped, tapped, tapped on the keyboard but glanced up when Ariel approached the window with hesitant steps. "Is anticipation what I see on your face?"

Ariel wiped her moist hands on her pants legs. "Just eager for the rest of the wedding party to join us."

Sierra guessed the nervous behavior had nothing to do with friends arriving for wine and cheese. "Gavin won't get drunk. Don't worry."

"You've never attended a SEAL wedding."

"Well no, but I'm certain Gavin would never disrespect you by participating, hungover, in his own wedding," she said as she continued typing. "Believe me, he can handle a rowdy night out with the boys."

Ariel drummed her fingers on the windowsill. "It's not Gavin I'm worried about."

"Weather alert," Sierra exclaimed once the local forecast flashed on the computer screen. "Oh, thank you, wind gods. Light to moderate breezes in the early afternoon tomorrow are expected."

Ariel's face lit up. "You've done it again."

"Done what?"

"Replaced my worry with your usual eagerness for anything resembling fun. For that, I'm chillin'."

"And I'm willing to help you do some chilling. All seriousness is hereby canceled. Turn on the music."

Ariel shimmied over to the blue tooth speaker and punched the on button. Sierra's cell phone blared the latest from Zumba's bimonthly training download.

With a crook of her index finger, Sierra called Ariel to the center of the room. "Help me create choreography for my upcoming master class."

The chorus of voices from downstairs interrupted Sierra's jubilation. "Four bridesmaids changed and ready to party," echoed through the house.

Sierra grabbed Ariel's wrist and tugged her down the stairs, plotting to distract her bestie with a few glasses of German wine and original dance moves choreographed to the newest Latin tunes. Anything to prevent Ariel from unnecessary worry about how Gavin was spending his evening.

I'm spending the night and will be available every minute of the wedding day for full moral support. If anything goes wrong, I'll be the first one to get notified and the one to solve any hiccup or full-blown disaster.

Chapter Three

"Hold him down, Pudge. I've got a straight razor in my hand," Tony urged his former platoon mate, as he lathered up Gavin's genitals.

Pudge Evanston's biceps bulged as he gripped the thick shoulders of the man lying beneath his hands, and struggled to hold him still. The man, zip-tied and supine on the hotel bed, had led them in combat and was a hero to most of the men but SEAL tradition overruled rank. When a navy SEAL got married, well…all bets were off, and all pranks went on overdrive.

"You're dead, Tony." Gavin seethed, his lips barely moving as he eyed the sharp edge of the blade.

Tony made a quick swipe along Gavin's groin. "I hear you brother," and wiped the excess shaving cream on a towel. "Cowboy, you and Gummer hold his legs," Tony barked at the other two SEALS in the room. "Pudge has the upper torso under control."

They complied, grinning like drunken sailors, each pressing a thigh into the mattress. The pre-wedding tradition might seem excessive or dark or even asinine to a civilian, but they all understood their time would come and as groomsmen, shaving his Johnson, was their duty.

Getting his friend drunk was easy, Tony mused. The all-too-willing female bartender snapped up the fifty to spike Gavin's tonic water with gin, the tasteless, odorless devil. Once he was stumbling drunk, they'd hauled him back to the hotel room, but a SEAL was still a SEAL, even shit-faced, as evidenced by the black bruise forming on Tony's eye and pain radiating to the back of his head.

"Ouch, Caveman" Tony said, using Gavin's SEAL team nickname as he took another swipe with the razor. "You slammed me with a right hook."

"You think that punch hurt? If I'm late for my wedding…let's just say, payback's a bitch."

Tony stretched the skin flat as he scraped the blade across Gavin's pubic region and slathered the excess dollop of cream and hair mixture on the cloth. "Almost done. You're gonna be so pretty, dude. Ariel will love your hairless dick."

Gavin hissed between gritted teeth as he zeroed in on Pudge, "I'm going to put Limburger cheese on your catalytic converter." He turned his head in a slight swivel and glared at the other two SEALs slurring, "I'll paint, 'sexual pervert' on the back windows of your trucks." He muttered a few more unintelligible threats as his eyelids fluttered in an effort to stay conscious.

Tony circled his fist in the air as Gavin's head lolled to the side and his body slumped, signaling the others it was time to roll. In one fluid movement, they wrapped a naked Gavin in the bedspread and picked him up in coffin formation. "Pudge, text Shoestring we have the package. Bring the car around."

Pudge, a short, compact SEAL with a few extra pounds of baby fat, asked, "Hey T-man, we gonna load him in the trunk?"

"Yeah, I don't think he'll wake up but just in case. It's a few hours' drive to the drop off point," Tony huffed as he stepped his way down the motel stairs, arms braced on Gavin's neck and shoulders.

Cowboy grunted, "Carrying Gavin, dead-drunk, takes me back to the damn IBS we bounced on our heads in BUDS every fucking place we walked."

"Don't you mean ran?" Tony asked the broad-shouldered Texan.

"The Inflatable Boat Small with room for seven trainees plus equipment doesn't define small." Gummer groaned and spat chewing tobacco. "But this is waaaay more fun than we had in training. Wish I had a hidden camera with sound to capture the moment when he wakes up."

A sleek four door limo idled at the curb; a tall, zero percent-body-fat male opened the driver's side door. "Pop the trunk, Shoestring." Tony said. He lowered the body in unity with the other two men, folding his legs to fit and added, "Sleep tight."

"He's gonna be pissed," Shoestring said, shaking his head as he tapped the close button on the trunk.

****

Someone had slammed a sledgehammer into his temple. While his head pounded like a bass drum, Gavin checked for blood. His hand returned covered in sweat but no blood.

Breathing a sigh of relief, he noticed the graffiti-decorated walls of a restroom surrounding him. "Where in Hell am I? Better find the guys." He fumbled for the cell phone in his cargo pants and grabbed the skin of his butt-ass naked body. *No shoes, no shirt, no nothing.*

"Ass-wipes." He uncurled from his slumped position on the toilet seat. "Payback is gonna be a bitch but first I need to find out out of here. No way I'm missing my own wedding."

Gavin shoved open the stall door and stumbled against the paper towel dispenser. He shouldered through the exit, clutching the paper towels partially covering his groin and lurched down a short, darkened hallway. As he weaved down the corridor, inhaling the smell of stale beer and sour urine, jukebox music served as a beacon for him to locate someone with a cell phone. He arrived at the entrance to the main room and took a cautious look around the doorjamb.

At least fifty tattooed, bearded males toting chained wallets gathered in small groups around a carved mahogany bar. All wore faded leathers adorned with skull and crossbones embroidered on the back. Waitresses, clad in halter tops and short, very short, cut-off jeans, mingled among the men, slapping at roving hands as they served beer.

Shit, a biker bar. Either I handle this or I'm going to die.

He stepped into the dim light. Fifty heads whipped around and stayed glued to his pale white ass as he squared his shoulders and strolled to the bar like he belonged there.

The bartender didn't lose a step as he continued drying a tall glass. "This resembles the first line of a joke," he mused, "a naked man walks into a bar…."

"Got a phone I can use?" Gavin asked, aware the group had migrated closer and formed a semi-circle around him.

The bartender nodded and picked up a cell phone and placed it on the bar. "Want a towel?"

"Appreciate it." Gavin answered with a sarcastic grin, holding up the tea-cloth sized dish towel the bar keep slid across the wood top.

A mountain-sized guy with bulging biceps, who Gavin guessed was the Alpha of the pack, tapped him on the shoulder. "What the fuck, dude? Are you on drugs or somethin'? This is our club and we don't like uninvited guests."

Gavin faced the barrel-chested Biker Boss with a calm demeanor. He didn't have a death wish and there was no reason to antagonize the guy. "No man. I'm getting married today. My friends—" He made quotation marks with his fingers. "—pranked me. Where in God's name am I?"

The biker's countenance remained hostile; his future actions unpredictable. The other members of the gang stayed vigilant but silent, in a pregnant wait for their pack leader to respond. As seconds ticked by in the stand-off, Gavin, with a rapid scan, assessed the availability of potential weapons. A beer bottle and a pool cue lay within reach. No clue if the bartender was packing heat behind the counter or whose side he might defend. He had to assume he was on his own. The single advantage was the element of surprise. A quick leap over the top of the bar and at least his family jewels would be out of the fray.

As Gavin rolled his body away from Biker Boss and positioned his wrists on the ledge, a chuckle erupted behind him. He glanced back and caught the leader pointing his index finger and shaking his head at Gavin's bare ass. One by one, the other males snickered, then openly jeered. The laughter spread, and the waitresses giggled in harmony, adding to the uproar. One even winked at him. The bartender sighed with apparent relief and offered him a beer.

"Thanks man, but no thanks." Gavin breathed an audible sigh and willed his heart to stop pounding against his chest.

Biker Boss clapped Gavin on the shoulder in a friendly gesture, "Dude, you're in our club bar, Fat Willies." He snapped his fingers at one of the men and indicated he needed the guy's pants. With quick compliance, the man yanked the cloth down his legs, as the boss continued, "Where and when's the wedding?"

"Horse farm outside of Ocala, this afternoon."

"Shit, man. You're in King's Bay, Georgia, more than a hundred miles up the interstate from where you need to be."

"As in King's Bay Naval Base?" Gavin asked, stunned by the revelation.

"Close. We're in the town near the naval base. You don't have much time. It's five a.m. and you have a two-and one-half-hour drive." He tossed the pants to Gavin. "Need us to give you a lift?"

In a one-handed catch, Gavin caught the tattered jeans mid-air and pictured himself seated shirtless, behind this bearded beast on a chopped Harley, roaring up the driveway to his family's home, minutes before his wedding. Then there was the matter of his new "friends." Would they expect an invitation to join the festivities? God, what a cluster-fuck.

"Appreciate the offer." Loosening his grip on the towel, which had provided scant cover, he let it fall to the floor. "What the hell. Too late to be embarrassed," he said as he yanked on the one-size-too-small pants. "Just need to make a call."

Gavin grabbed the offered cell phone and dialed the number for John Armstrong, his future brother-in-law. He punched the speaker button and listened to the rings, each one echoing into the next in an endless buzz. They had served together in Afghanistan until John got side-lined by an IED and ended up in a wheelchair with career-ending injuries. But instead of being bitter, he faced his circumstance with bravery and persisted on his road to recovery. He even signed up on a dating site.

The bikers returned to their round-robin joke telling and flirtations with the waitresses. Biker Boss remained at the bar, sipping his beer as if he wanted to ensure his new BFF connected with a ride home.

"Hello," John said after six long rings.

Finally. "Hey, bro, it's me." He covered creeping panic with a casual tone. "Did I wake you?"

"Are you kidding?" John's voice hitched. "Christ, Gavin, where are you?"

The distress in John's voice squeezed the already tight knot in his chest. "Biker bar near King's Bay Naval Base."

"Wait. What? In Georgia?"

Gavin snorted. "There's only one Kings Bay Naval Base, dude." He pressed the phone closer to his lips and lowered his voice, "Hey, have you talked to Ariel?"

"Um, well…yes."

No doubt I'm in deep shit. "How bad is it?"

"A lot of hand wringing and pacing…which you know is unlike my laid-back sister."

"I feel like such a heel." His shoulders slumped. "I should have seen this coming."

"It gets better."

"Great." Gavin muttered.

"The emotion evolved," he hesitated, obvious in his careful choice of words, "or devolved into livid swearing of your name after numerous unanswered messages to your voice mail. Sierra joined in, as only a best friend could, with flying finger texts and symbol rants to your phone."

"I get the picture." Gavin resigned himself to whatever reckoning was due him. *I need to get home, pronto.*

"The good news is after they exchanged ideas for your demise, Ariel fell asleep."

"Thank God she was able to sleep."

"I plied her with a couple of hot brandy toddies." John said. "And I talked Sierra out of driving to the hotel where the guys are staying which would not have ended well…for them."

Gavin completed a slow swipe down his face, mumbling, "I'm gonna kill those bastards."

"What? I didn't catch that."

"I said, don't wake Ariel but I need you to leave as fast as humanly possible and come pick me up. Roust one of the farm hands for help with driving. I don't want to sink deeper into trouble with your sister and my wife, as of tomorrow…I hope."

"No problem but shouldn't I call Tony to come with me? He's your best man."

"That prick is the reason I'm in this God forsaken place! I'll deal with him after the wedding. Just make sure he stays out of my way until then."

"Lord help him," John said. "What's the address of the—for God's sake you said biker bar, didn't you?" His voice pitched high from alarm. "Are you in immediate danger? I'll call the police."

Gavin punched the speaker button to off and held the phone tightly to his ear. He glanced at the bearded, tattooed man at his side currently engaged in casual conversation with the bartender and said urgently, "No. Definitely no police. It's cool. Here's the address, 2021 King's Bay Drive. You'll see about fifty, a majority Harleys, parked in front."

"Got it, Gav. Geez. Anything else?"

"Bring clothes."

John choked. "I don't even want to know.

****

Sierra rounded the corner into the kitchen as John's wheelchair started down the ramp of the back door. "Where are you going at this hour?"

John stopped the turning wheels and heaved a heavy sigh. "Shit!"

"Spill it."

"Gavin was kidnapped by Tony and the other groomsmen."

Sierra slapped the sides of her head. *No lo puedo creer*. "I can't believe it." Her gaze turned to John. "Unbelievable."

John nodded in agreement, "I'm leaving right now to get him."

"I'll get my purse and drive you."

"Not a good idea. He's naked in a biker bar."

Estupido. "Stupid. What a gang of idiots," she huffed. "While they were out having man-fun, Ariel cried herself to sleep, thinking her groom was missing and her wedding was ruined. She's a wreck, a sleeping wreck, mind you, but still a wreck."

"I get it and I totally understand. But the way to rectify all of this is to rescue Gavin and ensure he shows up for the wedding."

"You're right. What can I do to help?"

"Stay here. When Ariel wakes, reassure her Gavin will be back in time for the wedding. She has my word on it."

"Wait a minute. Back in time? It's eleven a.m. The biker bar is in Gainesville, correct?"

"Uh, no. The bar's in Georgia."

Sierra stomped her foot. "It's a five-hour round trip drive!" She raised her face to the heavens. *Yo lo Mato.* "I'll kill him and those lunatics he calls his friends."

John raised his eyebrows but grunted in response to the death threat. Silence was platinum in this case.

Chapter Four

The first day of May turned into a picture-perfect Florida day with temperatures kept in the mid-seventies by light sea breezes rolling inland. No stranger to this landscape, Sierra surveyed the rolling green hills hemmed by endless white picket fencing and concluded Wildwood Farms, the thoroughbred homestead where her best friend worked and lived, was the perfect venue for an outdoor wedding.

Under a canopy of oak trees, a custom-made wooden archway, with two barn doors as a cover, was draped in sheer white chiffon. Folding chairs, filled with friends and family chatting introductions, were covered in white linen and adorned with a combination of ivy and sprigs of Black-eyed Susans. Before lifting the bouquet of baby's breath and miniature pink roses, Sierra ran her hands down the short length of soft pink silk she wore and applauded Ariel's choice of bridesmaid's dresses. She sucked in a deep breath as the first skirl from a bagpipe signaled the start of the ceremony. The crowd shifted to their seats and sat in whispered anticipation. She eased a long exhalation.

Despite the over-the-top prank by the groom's SEAL buddies, happiness prevailed. Once Gavin explained what happened to him, then begged her forgiveness, Ariel, never one to hold a grudge, focused on the future. As Sierra waited for her musical cue, she observed the row of SEAL groomsmen lined up in sync with the bridesmaids, arms loose by their sides with attention on the spot where the groom would appear.

The one introduced to her as Pudge stretched in a catlike pose, calm and unruffled by the festivities. Cowboy, a Texas-grown former rodeo star, according to Gavin, said little but his blinding smile gave away his feelings. The one referred to as Shoestring didn't fit the prototype SEAL image until you witnessed the gracefulness of his every move. Gummer, famous for dipping chew tobacco, had a noticeably absent bulge inside his bottom lip. When she'd asked if Gummer was his real name, Gavin explained it was a nickname inspired by his premature, receding hairline which made him appear much older than his thirty-one years.

Christ! They could have been choirboys. Except Ariel's rundown of their lifestyle and the reckless nature of their pranking nixed the notion any of these men ever sang in a choir. She smiled to herself. *Ariel has no need to exact revenge on the bozo brigade because I'm going to do it for her.*

With a deep breath, she stepped into her assigned position as maid of honor in the bridal procession, determined to remain civil toward her partner, the best man and supreme asshole for almost screwing up Ariel's wedding. As the man approached, she squinted her eyes and did a double take. *No way. It couldn't be.*

As he edged closer, a puzzled frown crossed his face, then relaxed into a full smile of recognition. Finally, face to face they both said, "You!"

His sounded like a, happy to see you again 'you'.

Hers, she hoped, communicated a pissed-off to see you 'you'.

"Why didn't you call me?"

"You gave me drugs, remember? And when I took a shower…oh, what does it matter." She lowered her voice to a whispered seethe. "You kidnapped the groom. I'm glad I didn't call you."

The procession music pitched louder. The maid of honor glanced over the crowd and realized all eyes focused on them. Tony offered her a dimpled grin and extended an elbow. With a fixed forward glare, she placed her rigid palm on his forearm as they awaited their musical cue. "How could you?" she said between stiff but smiling lips.

"Hey, it's all good." Tony grinned, deepening his dimple. "He's here, isn't he?"

"No thanks to you and your merry band of juvenile idiots."

"Now, now. No need for name calling." He gave her hand a gentle pat. "It's a SEAL tradition, B-a-b-y." With a cavalier nod toward the cowgirl boots she and all the bridesmaids wore, he said, "Nice boots."

Exasperated and feeling as though she'd been smacked on the behind, Sierra vowed to have the last word with Mr. Towering Ego. *While everyone is busy eating and chugging at the reception and after I've had a few glasses of wine, Tony Franco is going to get several pieces of my mind.*

The bagpipe's skirl ended, and the first notes of ethereal harp music floated through the air. A lump rose in Sierra's throat as Wager, the family Border Collie, trotted down the aisle, a small white basket clenched in his teeth. Two rings glistened atop a satin cushion stuffed inside. The beloved dog had originally brought Ariel and Gavin together, so ring bearer was a fitting position for the cute pooch. He wagged his tail all the way to the end of the runway and released his hold on the container as Gavin joined him, approaching from the side. With his ears forward and alert, the dog's head faced the next couple in the wedding party as they stepped in cadence with the music, toward the groom.

Three more couples traversed the flower-strewn pathway. It was almost time for the expectant crowd to capture the first vision of the breathtaking and beautiful bride. Sierra's heart fluttered with excitement for her friend and she sneaked a peek backwards to see if Ariel was in sight but a sharp tug on her arm jerked her forward and she stumbled on the carpeted runway. A strong arm wrapped around her waist and steadied her.

"You're welcome," Tony breathed in her ear.

Sierra flashed a bright smile as she passed the attendees, wondering if the steam billowing from her ears was as visible as the spread of heat across her face. "Arrogant ass," she hissed in reply, keeping her eyes focused ahead.

They arrived at the front of the main aisle where they would each shift to their respective sides. Before Tony could release her arm, she jerked free from his grip and slid to the left. He shifted right and peered at her with a relaxed half smile. Nothing fazes him, she fumed, infuriated at his nonchalance.

A few seconds of silence passed before everyone stood as the first few notes of the "Bridal March" pulsed in vibrant rhythm. Heads rotated in unison. A few dramatic gasps layered the air as Ariel, a vision in flowing alabaster and coral roses, appeared next to her escort, her brother, John. The glowing bride placed her hand on his shoulder as he pressed the button of his motorized wheelchair. Together they proceeded forward, nodding and smiling as they passed the onlookers, the women with hands clasped in obvious joy and the men in evident admiration. Radiant and poised, Ariel fixed her gaze on Gavin, her future husband, who beamed with uninhibited enthusiasm.

Intermittent sniffles served as a subtle background while the minister recited the couple's own penned vows. Sierra's eyes brimmed with tears as her dearest friend said, "I do." She glanced at Tony, gauging his response to his best friend's commitment to love and cherish and was met with an intentional wink.

What does that imply? Is this a joke to him? She rolled her eyes in response. "Ass-wipe," she mouthed as they linked arms and fell in behind the new Mr. and Mrs. Cross.

****

The crowd followed the newlyweds down a manicured pathway lighted by antique lanterns to a nearby tent that served as the reception location. Miniature lights strung in neat rows along each metal beam added to the festive mood as did the music already blaring from inside. Tony made his way toward the commotion in the center of the removable wooden dance floor, while his mind idled on the breaking news he was being hunted.

No way would he tell Gavin or his SEAL friends about his Wanted: Tortured Until Death status. Not here, not now. He'd need to shore up his perimeter after he arrived back home on the coast and install extra security. What he needed now was stress relief. As he wedged his way into the man circle formed around the bride and several of her bridesmaids, his gaze locked on the curvy whirlwind in the center of the fun.

Her hair, pinned up in a bun for the wedding, now cascaded in thick waves down her back. Sweat pearled on her forehead, a result of the gyrating hips and boob shimmies, no doubt. All the men clapped their approval and egged the ladies on, some shouting, "Get low," others ordering, "Booty shake," with a few gratuitous, "Take it offs."

C'mon, guys. Take it off? Really? His hands slammed together, stinging from repetition but he stifled the urge to act like he was in a strip club.

Someone yelled, "Conga line." With Sierra in the lead, the bridesmaids fell in behind her. As they snaked past him, he jumped in, gripping the jiggling lower body of one of the bridesmaids. She cut him a bright flirtatious smile and waved a welcome to the rest of the guys. They leap-frogged into the meandering dance line with the precision of SEALS executing a combat insertion.

Party on.

****

Covered in sweat, Sierra swiped her brow as she secretly checked out the best man twirling his flawless, sculpted arms above his head in a half circle in front of her. She had to hand it to Tony. He was gifted with natural rhythm although she maintained he was still an ass-wipe who could dance seamlessly picked up on Zumba basics. A definite plus in her book of likes, not to mention his mad nursing skills, but a couple of positives didn't cancel the plethora of arrogant synonyms which stretched out in her mind like a kitten with a roll of toilet paper. The DJ ended the music and announced the cake cutting.

As Gavin and Ariel hand fed each other a piece of cake, Sierra observed Tony's unreadable features and wondered if anything ever elicited a reaction in him. His "whoop, whoop" with the rest of the guests on completion of the cake face-stuffing came across as genuine but…the announcement of the respective garter and bouquet toss interrupted her thoughts.

While the crowd swarmed toward the bride and groom, Sierra sashayed in the opposite direction toward the edge of the platform where she hoped to dodge the bouquet toss by cozying up to a glass of champagne. With her hand outstretched toward the bartender, satisfied she'd accomplished her feat, she curled her lips in a smug smile. *Catastrophe avoided.*

Tony grabbed her free hand and tugged her toward the gathering crowd. "Going my way?"

Caught off guard, she jerked her hand back but couldn't escape his strong grasp. "Wait."

With an infectious grin and using his index finger as a pointer, Tony indicated the group of women clustered in front of the bride and said, "Don't you want to join the fun?"

In a feeble attempt to resist, she added, "My champagne."

Tony initiated a full circle, whisking the glass of bubbly out of the bartender's hand and thrusting the stem in her palm before resuming his course to the front of the gathered crowd.

"Nice move," she muttered over the lip of the glass, then sipped a taste.

His smile reached his eyes as he wrapped his arm around her waist and snugged her to his side. "Oh, I'm just getting started." With his lips touching her ear he whispered, "I'm not the asshole you think I am."

Sierra gulped the rest of the liquid nectar, her ears buzzing from either the champagne or the heat blossoming between her legs from the proximity of the super-hot nurse, SEAL and flirtatious best man. Distracted, she missed seeing the copious bouquet of coral and white roses intermingled with baby's breath as it plummeted straight for her face.

From somewhere in the crowd, a feminine squeal jerked her attention skyward, "Sierra, catch it."

Instinctively, she leaped straight up, her arm extended with fingers splayed until the ends of a satin bow draped her hand. Velvet petals from the roses brushed her cheek as she captured the stem and secured the flowers in her grip.

Oh my God. I caught the bouquet. Now what?

As if in answer to her musing, Tony stepped into view, his wide palm outstretched, filling the air space as a blue garter appeared, descending like a frilly comet. Then it disappeared. *Who caught it?* She perused the males hovered in a semi-circle.

"Whew." Tony separated from the crowd and clutched the garter in a triumphant wave. He started toward Sierra, a shit-eating grin covering his face.

She returned the smile. *Of course, he caught the garter.* Her gaze shifted to stare blankly at the clump of flowers in her hand.

"Nice catch." He dangled the cloth in the air and then smoothed his arm around her waist. "I guess you're the one I put this on."

"Reflex reaction," she said, removing his arm as if it were a smelly sock. "Not a chance you're sliding a garter on my thigh."

She handed him the arrangement before stalking to the buffet table, although food was the last thing on her mind. The music resumed and drowned out his no doubt, smart-assed reply. *What a jag-off. But what a hot, exciting, funny jag-off.*

One of her favorite Salsa tunes came on and the other bridesmaids called her name to join them. She sidestepped in rhythm on to the dance floor her arms looping around her waist in perfect small circles. Ariel joined her along with the other female party-goers and formed lines behind Sierra, imitating her every step.

The music stopped, and the DJ announced it was time to put on the garter. *What? Was she really going to allow him to grab her thigh?* She leaned toward Ariel and mouthed, "Have to pee," before she bolted off the dance floor.

Rushing to catch her best friend, Ariel called, "Hey Sierra, wait a minute. Time to don the garter…do you honestly have to pee or is this about something?" She cocked a brow. "Or someone?"

Caught in a selfish impulse, Sierra realized rather than make a scene; she'd go through with the ridiculous custom for her most cherished friend. "I was escaping. Your husband's friend gives me the jitters."

"Jitters as in you'd like to hold the beautiful jellyfish, but you might get stung?"

Withholding the snarky comment that popped into her head, Sierra put her arm through Ariel's and turned them toward the stage. "I'm good. Let's do this."

Ariel hugged her closer and sighed. "Thanks."

Wolf whistles and catcalls drowned out Tony's words as he lifted Sierra's dress high on her thigh. She sucked in her breath as his hand skimmed the inside of her leg. Goosebumps popped up along her arms and the pit of her stomach somersaulted. She gazed at the top of his uncovered head, fixated on the thick layers of textured hair while he adjusted the garter a few inches above her knee. With an uncontrollable urge to massage the deep brown mop, she scrunched and poised her fingers an inch from contact but froze when he raised his head and locked eyes with her. *Did he have x-ray vision?* She gasped, dropped her arms, and plopped her hands in her lap.

His eyes, almost black with intensity, messaged clear desire as he offered his hand. "Want to dance?"

Her nipples hardened and moisture dampened her thighs. "Sure," she squeaked.

The notes of a slow song drifted across the dance floor. *No pressure, no pressure, no pressure*. She stepped onto the platform and was hugged into a ripped chest. Engulfed by the musk scent, she laid her head on his shoulder, her nose pressed into his warm neck. The silence screamed while their feet shuffled together across the floor without missing a beat. The song ended too soon. *Aren't there more lyrics?*

As they drew apart, Tony said, "Thanks." And offered a smoldering look. "Am I forgiven?"

Ay dios mio. I'm a goner.

Chapter Five

Two days later, Tony boarded a plane out of Tampa for the return flight to LA without telling the other SEALS about his predicament. He didn't have the heart to ruin his best friend's bliss. As the attendant greeted him, he scanned the faces of a preoccupied businessmen, a mother coping with a fussy infant and a group of tourists with T-shirts stamped, 'I Visited Key West', searching for jihadists hell-bent on killing him.

Condition Yellow, he concluded. Stay alert; no imminent danger.

His shoulders relaxed and drooped forward as he shuffled to the back of the plane and located his seat. After stuffing his duffel bag in the overhead bin, he eased into his preferred aisle position. Nodding to the cute college girl on his right, he shut down his phone and settled in for the long flight home while reading his favorite author.

Jarred awake by the thud of the plane's wheels as they hit the tarmac, Tony jerked upright and peered out the small window to his right. He grabbed his bag from the overhead after helping the young girl who sat next to him haul her overstuffed bag to the ground. After making his way through the crowds with the deftness of an athlete, he exited street level and immediately wished he could tele-port back to Florida where the air smelled fresh, not clogged with gas fumes.

He zigzagged across the six lanes of slow but steadily moving traffic before entering the parking garage where he paused to scan the perimeter. So far so good…and there's my car, right where I left it. After tossing his bag in the back seat, he unlocked the glove compartment, withdrew his 9mm, placed it on the bucket seat beside him, and covered it with a towel. Ten minutes later he zipped into the I-405 traffic, laboring through the bowels of the overcrowded city.

He checked his phone, hoping for a call from Sierra. He had scrawled his phone number on the garter. Nothing from her yet, but the flush of pink on her cheeks when he slipped the garter belt up her thigh was unmistakable. She'd call.

After forty-five minutes of a bumper to bumper, stop and go crawl along the I-405, he whipped right onto the Wilshire Blvd exit and within a few minutes turned into the garage of his Westwood apartment. He leaned forward and with precaution, stuck the weapon in his back waistband, underneath his shirt tail. Loaded down with his duffel bag and computer case, he stepped onto the elevator and punched the number three.

A short ride later, the door slid open and he strode the few steps to his apartment. As soon as he stuck the key in the lock and opened the door, his sense of danger spiked. Fine hairs on the back of his neck stood on end. *Someone's been in my apartment…or, is still here.*

In a bowling ball motion, he tossed the duffel bag against the living room wall before stepping inside and drawing his gun. Keeping it at the ready, he used his right foot to close the door while he eased his computer bag off his shoulder and laid it on the carpet. Reaching back with his left hand, he locked the door behind him.

No perps in or out.

The nautical clock he kept on his appointment book had been shifted. Heart thumping hard against his rib cage, he reached the desk on the other side of his living room in three easy strides. *Where is the tell?* He always placed a strand of hair under the clock and faced the clock an inch to the left. The hair was missing, and the clock was twisted to the right.

Jesus! His neck muscles tensed. A tight band of pressure squeezed his forehead. *No sign of forced entry What the hell is going on?*

His selected ring tone, "Bad to the Bone" belted out of his cell phone and for a split second, jarred his attention. He glanced at the caller ID. *Sierra? Talk about timing.*

He ignored the call and the subsequent notification beep for voice mail but realized anyone still in the apartment was now alerted. He assumed the crouched position for clearing a room. Hyper-aware, his senses extended to perceive any shadows, smells, or sounds, as he maneuvered systematically from room to room scanning for anything missing or out of place.

Window locks jimmied? No. And nothing missing. His appointment book appeared to be their only interest, but why didn't they take it? Because whoever it was didn't want to be detected. Not the typical B&E. The recent warning from his former SEAL leader flashed through his mind in neon colors. Could the jihadis have found him this soon?

It seemed unlikely but not wanting to take any chances, he grabbed his car keys, and headed for the local spy store where he could purchase a bug detector kit. Taking extra precaution, he parked his car in a nearby alley littered with empty cardboard boxes and slipped into the back door of the shop owned by his trusted friend.

Spotless with a slight odor of floor wax, the inside reflected the military organization of its owner. Items hung on the cream-colored walls, neatly grouped by their usage. Glass cases filled with high-end cameras, microphones and state of the art bug detectors, lined the walls. The owner glanced up and acknowledged him with a short nod before thanking his customer for their business. Tony stepped to one side, concentrating on the low hum of music from a local rock station until the customer exited.

"Hey, Pudge," he joked, glancing toward the door. "Long time no see."

"Very funny, smart-ass. You just get back?"

"Yeah. Hey man, I got a problem." He scanned the walls behind the counter. "Need your help."

"Anything. Name it."

"Someone broke into my apartment while I was in Ocala. I need a bug detector kit."

"Wait a minute." Pudge stepped to the front door and locked the deadbolt, flipped the open sign to read, closed and pulled down the canvas blind. "Did they steal anything? Why a bug detector kit?"

"Nothing's missing. That's the problem."

Pudge frowned. "What aren't you telling me?"

A slow smile ascended across Tony's lips. "You always were a master interrogator. My personal defense system was violated."

"The string and the book or is it the hair and cup?"

"The hair was missing, and the clock was out of position, smart ass."

"Jesus, dude. That's messed up." Pudge grabbed Tony's arm and steered him to the camera section. "We need to set up cameras in case they come back."

"Not a bad idea. I'd like to get a face to go along with the threat."

"Someone threatened *you*? Brother, you better give it up because my bullshit meter is on high alert."

"Let's grab the cameras and the bug detector. I'll tell you everything on the ride back to my apartment."

He crossed his arms and braced his left foot against the wall, a stubborn frown covered his face. "Not so fast T-man. The equipment we take depends on who's after your ass so I'm not moving a centimeter until you tell me who we're up against." Pudge was a guy who could wait eons for an answer.

"A ghost from the past," Tony said.

Chapter Six

Sierra checked the screen of her cell phone. No missed calls. Nothing. *It's been hours since I left a message.* Frustrated, she stuffed the mobile device in her gear bag and inhaled a deep breath.

Up next: instructing a few hundred excited Los Angeles Zumba followers in a fast-paced Salsa. At the top of her game, Sierra routinely received invitations from well-known instructors who taught all over the U.S. to be the headliner in their Master Class. Today, was no exception. Her routine had to be flawless. Any distraction could cause a misstep and cuing the crowd to step left as she sailed right. *Not going to happen.*

In an expression of faith, she crossed herself, forehead to chest, shoulder to shoulder. As the announcer's voice boomed her name through the speaker system of the convention center, chills skittered down her arms. She shook off the nerves and burst onto the stage, hands stretched above her head, clapping in rhythm to the music. As she high-stepped to the center of the stage, the cheering crowd mimicked her movements. A sea of bright pastel colors and hundreds of ponytails mirrored her sassy routine. Drops of sweat rolled from her scalp and soaked the purple headband she wore. Her heart rate soared. She loved being in the zone.

The song ended in what seemed like a few seconds

after it began. Sierra was whisked off the stage as another instructor entered. Someone handed her a towel and a bottle of water as she made her way to the dressing area. She dug into her bag and retrieved her cell. *Still no message.*

What's up with that? She was only in LA for another twenty-four hours and then had to return to Florida. *It's now or never, Tony Franco. Your big chance to have coffee with 'moi' and convince me you're not the asshole I think you are, is about to lapse.*

Thinking Ariel could offer insight into his hot and cold act, Sierra tapped in her best friend's number and waited for the sweet southern drawl on the other end.

"Hello Sierra. How's the conference? Fun?"

"Understatement, my friend. Hey, I called Mr. Dancing Fool hours ago and left a voice mail but nothing, *nada*."

Ariel snorted. "Dancing, agreed. But fool? Only if he doesn't call you back. Gavin has told me he works odd hours. He most likely had an emergency at the hospital. Don't read anything into the lack of response. I guarantee he'll be executing back flips on his surfboard when he realizes you called."

"Surfing is on his resume?" Sierra grunted. "Ugh."

"You don't like surfers or surfing, what?"

"One more thing we don't have in common."

"Sierra, the ball's in your court. According to my husband and I do love saying *husband*, Tony is smitten. I see no harm in calling him while you're in LA."

"I left a voice mail, asking him to meet for coffee."

Ariel chuckled. "Well, coffee is something you have in common. And Sierra?"

"Yes?"

"Tony's not a man who drinks cold coffee. I'm fairly sure he likes it hot."

"OMG. You are such a newlywed horn dog. Go accost your husband or something."

"Good luck. I'm glad you didn't wash the garter."

"Hanging up now." She punched off and shook her head with a laugh. Ariel was the first real friend she made when she relocated to the States. After years of confessing secrets, sharing problems and supporting each other through disappointments, they were closer than sisters.

With growing curiosity about Tony, she hoped he would her before she left town. She gathered her things and stuffed them into her oversized tote. After a quick glance in the mirror to check for any mascara drip, Sierra joined several of the other instructors chatting about where to eat lunch.

"I know a cozy little place on the way to the airport," she offered. "It has great coffee."

Chapter Seven

Pudge shook his head in disbelief. "ISIS is hunting *you*? Here? In the states?" He stared at Tony as if waiting for the punch line. "You got to be shitting me."

"Not shitting you. Our old XO paid me a visit to deliver a warning to stay low and watch my back. Apparently, there's a bounty on my head."

"Dude, that's intense. Why you?"

"I treated a guy at a CIA black site who happened to be the son of a sheik and—"

Pudge interrupted, "Let me guess. He died?"

"Not while I worked on him. He was alive when I left." Tony raised his head to witness the understanding blossom on Pudge's face.

"Hey man, you can't stay at your apartment. Pack your shit. You're coming home with me."

"I'm not hiding, Pudge. I acted like a total wimp in high school. The days of anyone besting me are over."

"What do you mean, acted like a wimp?"

"I was the new kid and a late bloomer. The shy, skinny kid with no social skills or friends." He huffed. "Which put a target on my back for the Neanderthals who wanted to beat the snot out of me…if they could catch me before I arrived at the bus stop. It's how I learned to run."

Pudge gave his friend's arm a mock punch. "Check out the bright side. You're such a good runner, no one in BUDS could beat your four-mile run time in sand. Last I heard, you still hold the record."

Tony scoffed. "Born from necessity."

"Well, born from necessity, we're calling the team. You're not going solo, man."

Tony made a heart sign over his chest with a clear intention of sarcasm. "Aww, you love me."

"I don't want to pay for your funeral, asshole." Pudge shouldered past him to the door. "Get the lead out. We can set up the surveillance and be gone in less than an hour. Oh, and call Gavin. I'll drive."

Tony eyed his phone and noticed the missed call with a Florida exchange. *Shit*. With all the excitement of the breakin, he'd forgotten about the message. His bottom jaw dropped as he listened to his voice mail. *Sierra? In LA? And wants to have coffee. Am I dreaming?*

He glanced at Pudge. *No way I'm calling her with prying ears present and subject myself to pokes and jabs, ad infinitum.* He stared out the windshield. *When I'm alone in my room at Pudge's house....*

He scrolled through the numbers until he located Gavin's contact info and tapped the phone symbol. After two rings, he hit the end call button. "Pudge, what if my phone is tapped…or they can ping it?"

The former SEAL's head whipped around. "Turn your phone off, take out the battery and no more calls on that phone. We'll buy you a prepaid using cash."

"Good call, my brother." Pudge had reverted into all business, operator mode. No need to bore him with the details but he had to find a way to call Sierra back.

"I'll phone Gavin after we have you safely stowed at my house." Pudge said.

Blanketed in the shadows of night, the two SEALs installed the security cameras at Tony's apartment. Upon completion of a second check of the interior Tony determined there'd been no further incursions and began packing his belongings, not sure when he'd be able to return. After zigzagging through LA traffic and negotiating numerous detours designed to misdirect any pursuers, they arrived at Pudge's house at midnight.

Too tired to do anything but sleep, Tony promised himself he'd procure a burner phone first thing in the morning, then call Sierra. Regardless of being hunted by hired killers, he'd find a way to spend time with the sexy dance instructor.

"Wake up sleeping beauty," Pudge called. "It's almost zero eight hundred and we have work to do to save your sorry ass."

Startled to realize how late he'd slept and with the window of opportunity to connect with Sierra closing, Tony spat, "We need to get a burner phone, pronto."

"First things first. I spoke to Gavin. How much leave time do you have saved up?"

"Other than the days I took for the wedding, I haven't used any, so almost three weeks. Why?"

"We have to get you out of town and to his farm in Florida where you have cover until we locate the creepers. "They'll be on *our* turf then."

"Forget it." Tony clenched his jaw. "No way am I putting Gavin and his family at risk."

The creases in Pudge's brow deepened. "Then what do you suggest? Shelter in place at my house?"

"No. It's business as usual." Tony scraped his hands through his cropped hair. "Listen man, I appreciate you and Gavin having my back, but the trauma center is already short-handed. If I disappear, the workload dumps on my coworkers who are already overloaded. In fact, I have to go in today for a few hours to cover for one of them."

"What if you're dead, T-man? Who benefits then?"

"I'll think about it." Tony exhaled a heavy audible sigh. "I've worked so hard to put my life in order, to have a career after the SEAL teams. Now this."

Pudge nodded. "I get it. I do, man. We'll have this wrapped up in short order and life will go on."

"Anyway we could leave Gavin out of this?"

"Not on your life. He's already called one of his hunting buddies who works as a deputy at the Marion County sheriff's office for possible backup."

"Why don't we call in the FBI while we're at it?"

"Excellent idea. I'll get right on it."

"You're an annoying prick."

A shit-eating grain capturing Pudge's face. "Glad to be of service."

Tony glanced at his watch, blocking any tells as panic surged in his veins. Another hour had zipped by. He didn't know the departure time of Sierra's flight, but he hoped she opted for the red-eye. "Give me a lift to the closest Walmart so I can buy a phone."

"Sure. There's one near my store."

"I parked my car in the alley behind your shop. Drop me off and I'll pick up the phone on my own."

"Then what?"

"I work the added shift at the hospital," Tony said, observing Pudge's infectious cheer turn to a frown. Heck, the guy was honestly worried about him. "I'll call you when I'm in my car on my way back. Deal?"

"Deal, bro."

****

With his new prepaid phone positioned in his lap, Tony punched in Sierra's number, hit the speaker button and exited into traffic. The first ring, silence echoed, the second ring, dead air. Tony tightened his jaw and muttered, "Pick up, pick up…."

"Hello?"

The familiar honey-covered voice caressed his ear. "Sierra. Do you still have time for dinner? When does your flight take off?"

"I'm leaving on the red-eye and it was coffee." She chuckled. "Dinner ups the ante. Pretty slick maneuver."

"Okay. Coffee and dessert?"

"You don't give up, do you?"

"Never give up, never quit, the SEAL credo."

"Yeah, okay, but I think that credo refers to the battlefield."

"Haven't you ever listened to the song, 'Love is a Battlefield'?"

Sierra laughed. "I surrender. Where and when?"

"How about I pick you up at five, packed and travel-ready at your hotel? We'll grab a bite and I'll give you a lift to the airport."

"Sounds good. I'm staying at the Aventura hotel, downtown."

"Perfect. I'm familiar with the area. See ya then."

****

After a single conversation with Sierra, Tony's mood spiked from grim worry to eager anticipation. He operated on automatic as he parked his car on the fifth level of the Southern Cal Med Center. Mentally, he was stoked by an unexpected opportunity to spend time with Sierra. He headed for the card reader and check-in at security with a brisker than usual gait prompted by the idea of a single afternoon standing between him and a very hot woman.

With a nod to Fred, the under-qualified and unarmed security officer, he validated his decision to tuck his 9mm handgun inside his fanny pack. *Gun free zone be damned when I'm hunted by unidentified bad guys.* He returned the smile offered by the guard.

As emergencies poured in, Tony found himself elbow deep in cuts, burns and broken bones. Detached from the ominous personal threat lurking outside the sterile emergency room environment, he focused on the suture needle as it pierced the skin, then tugging the thread through the other side and using the forceps to tie a final knot. "Your arm should heal without a problem," he said smiling, as he patted the young boy's shoulder. "Might be wise to leave rescuing cats stuck in treetops to the fire department, though."

The boy's mother didn't give her son a chance to answer. "Count on it."

Tony glanced at the wall clock, suddenly aware of the shift change. While an orderly made the room ready for the next patient, he stripped off his surgical gloves and tossed them in the red biological waste container. He grabbed his tablet, filled in the notes from the last patient and hung it on the wall next to the double swinging metal doors.

"Goodnight Mr. Franco," the orderly called.

"Goodnight," Tony answered as he nudged the door open with his hip.

Pulse quickening, he hurried toward the locker room cognizant it was only two hours before the surrounding green walls would convert into a vision of

Sierra loveliness. After a record setting shower, he threw on his pants and dress shirt, then hurried to the dimly lit parking garage and jogged to his car. Although it was only minutes past four in the afternoon, this level of the parking area appeared dark and deserted.

Uneasiness gurgled in his stomach as he glanced around. Nothing appeared out of place. So many available spaces this time of night made sense. The evening shift staff was a skeleton crew, so most of them parked on the lower levels.

The hair on his neck sprung up and a tingle shimmied down his spine. A quick glance at his watch told him he didn't have time to waste but his instincts were rarely wrong, so he went to one knee to check under the carriage of his car. *No bombs. That's a relief.*

He stood and with a quick swipe, dusted off his pants before opening the driver's door. Reaching under the dash, he felt for the front hood latch and popped it. Not sure what to look for, he peered under the hood and scanned for anything jimmied, twisted or cut. *Nothing appears out of place or missing.*

He breathed a deep sigh as he slid into the front seat, lifted the gun out of his pouch and placed it under the newspaper on the seat next to him. The key turned with ease and the engine purred to life. Relaxed, he shifted the car into gear and rolled down the first ramp, picking up speed. He tapped the brakes, but the vehicle only gained momentum as it wound inside the concrete barriers. Tony pressed hard on the brake but instead of stopping, the car careened, unaffected, toward the exit.

"Shit!" His fingers wrapped in a tight grip around the steering wheel as his mind scrambled for solutions. He pumped the pedal one final time while downshifting to slow the runaway car. The station wagon strained as gravity propelled it toward Westwood Boulevard, the busy four-lane street that intersected with the garage exit ramp. Sweat beaded Tony's forehead. If the car entered the street at thirty MPH, he'd most likely hit one or more automobiles, maybe pedestrians. The impact would doubtless injure him, or worse, maim or harm innocent people.

The opening to the street loomed ahead. No other option. His jaw set in a hard line; Tony braced himself before reaching for the parking brake. He yanked, aiming the front bumper for the center of the concrete wall bordering the exit. The deafening screech of metal colliding with concrete jammed his ears. A loud boom and the air bag deployed, slamming into his chest, whip-lashing his head back and forth as the car thudded to a halt. He fought to maintain consciousness as he grabbed for the door handle, but a curtain of black fuzziness descended. His world sank into darkness.

Chapter Eight

Tony struggled for his weapon while octopus-like hands pinned him to the flat surface. As he rose through murky layers of thick mental fog, he writhed and flailed in an attempt at freedom. Gradually, his vision cleared. The blurry forms that restrained him formed faces. All looked scared.

He froze. He was in his own emergency room, surrounded by alarmed coworkers…as the patient. No need for his gun, especially since he didn't have it anyway. Instinctively, his hand reached toward the searing pain that sliced through his forehead. "Ouch!"

A familiar drawl sounded in the midst of the unintelligible babble surrounding him. "Easy cowboy."

"Pudge, what the hell?"

He tried to raise his head and locate his friend, tried to focus. Crushing pain throbbed from temple to temple. To control the agony, he inhaled deep, slow, even breaths through his nose, and then exhaled in a burst. In, out, in out. Although he worked in a hospital and had become desensitized to the antiseptic stench, today was different. The smell made him want to puke. As he tried to manage his roiling stomach, a familiar scent of citrus aftershave wafted up his nostrils.

Pudge leaned in close to his ear and whispered, "Dude, you crashed your car into a retaining wall on the exit ramp of the hospital garage. What happened?"

"Ahhhhh. Brakes. Didn't work. Couldn't stop. Did I, was anyone…?"

"You're good, brother. Thanks to quick thinking and plowing the front bumper of your car into a concrete barrier, you didn't careen onto the city street and take out a few pedestrians. One of your shift buddies, who heard the crash, called me and after he had you taken to the emergency room, removed certain . . . items from your car."

Pudge raised his eyebrows in a 'you get my drift?' look. "You're one lucky bastard. He arrived within seconds of the accident and prevented unwanted—" He stroked his chin and squinted. "—interference. If he hadn't, you'd have more than a lump on your head."

Tony tapped the side of his head with his index finger. "Yeah, man. Tracking."

"I know how meticulous you are about maintaining your car. Somebody fucked with the brakes."

"The idea did occur to me." He touched the side of his head and winced. "Police?"

"I see no reason to involve them at this point."

"Good idea. My insurance company can handle any damage to the hospital property."

"We need to boogie. You're not safe here."

"What about my car?"

"Made arrangements with a buddy who owns an auto repair shop. He'll tow it to his place and will check it out." Shifting his balance from one foot to the other, Pudge asked, "Can you walk?"

Tony raised himself off the exam table, bracing both arms to steady himself. The ER doc raced over. "You might have a concussion, bro. You need to rest."

"Pudge," Tony said, angling a thumb toward his

friend, "has experience with treating head injuries. I'm in capable hands. Will you sign me out, Doc?" He swung his legs off the table and gingerly planted his feet on the floor. "Please."

"You can sign yourself out, but I don't recommended it."

Pudge hoisted Tony's arm across his thick shoulder and secured his muscular forearm around his friend's waist. "Where's the release form?"

With a sigh of resignation, the doctor leveled the computerized tablet at Tony's chest. Pudge steadied it while Tony signed the attached form with the attached pen. "Thanks Doc," Pudge said. "Tony has decided to use his backlogged vacation time, starting now."

"I can arrange the time off but what's going on, you two?"

"That accident was no accident," Pudge replied stone-faced.

Tony interjected, "Trust me on this, Doc. For your own safety, don't ask any questions."

"We gotta go. Pronto." Pudge tugged Tony through the emergency room exit and maneuvered him the short distance to the rear loading dock of the hospital.

"We're officially ghosts," Tony muttered as they slid through the archway and vanished into the night.

Chapter Nine

The conveyor belt groaned and jerked, signaling another spectacle of suitcases, tossed atop the revolving metal plates, would soon trundle out for capture by waiting travelers. Sierra leaned forward, eager for a view of her bright red bag, the one with a Zumba sticker plastered on the side for easy identification.

Cranky about the early hour and lack of sleep on the overnight flight home, she grumbled to the stranger standing next to her, "My bag was put on board last minute. I almost missed my flight." *Thank you, Tony Franco.* "Shouldn't it be first out of the chute?"

The stranger smiled and nodded. "You'd think so but maybe the bag was loaded on a later flight."

Sierra groaned. "I live in Gainesville and have a two-hour drive home *after* I get my bag."

"Good luck," he said as he hoisted a black nylon bag from the revolving belt.

The suitcases and passengers from the LA flight thinned out until only a few people waited. Sierra's earlier sarcasm evolved into internal fuming. *What was I thinking to buy into the smooth-talking SEAL dude's player pitch? Well, lesson learned. That's for sure.*

A flash of red emerged through the plastic flaps on the conveyor and caught Sierra's eye as a wave of relief swept through her. "Thank God."

Not waiting for the bag to reach her position, she

lurched sideways, clutched the handle and swung the heavy suitcase onto the floor.

Within thirty minutes, aided by single-minded focus on the comforts of home, Sierra found herself zigzagging through four lanes of morning traffic as she steered toward the I-275 north exit. Once on the interstate, cruising with the steady flow of cars and trucks, she checked her watch. At eight a.m. Ariel would be making her rounds but Sierra needed to vent. With one eye on the road, she tapped the favorite's icon which brought up her best friend's avatar on the hands-free option on the car's dash.

The phone rang three times while she drummed her fingers in a fast staccato on the steering wheel. Ariel's cheerfulness sounded in her ear with a welcomed familiarity. "Girlfriend. Back from globetrotting?"

"Yeah. My plane landed right on time at seven o'clock this morning and I'm in my car driving back. Umm, you got a minute?" Her hand trembled as she clutched the steering wheel.

"Sure. Hold a sec while I remove my dirty gloves."

"I figured you'd be in the barn with the horses," she said, trying to steady her wavering voice.

"Everything okay? I'm not hearing the usual chipper in your voice. More like not so great, or WTF."

"He never showed. We had a date for coffee, which, aided by his persuasive skills, morphed into dinner, dessert and coffee but…. he didn't even call to cancel. What the hell, Ariel?"

"I assume we're talking about Tony?"

"Who acts like this? Are we in high school? I almost missed my flight waiting for him to show up or call. What a douche bag."

"Okay, I'm filling in the douche bag blank with the name, Tony Franco."

"Noooooo. I'm the douche bag for buying his load of B.S." Sierra snapped her head with a vigorous shake. "Funny thing…he seemed so sincere, like he was really interested. I don't get it."

"I'm sure there's an explanation, Sierra. I don't know him all that well, but Gavin does. They've been friends since college and from what he's told me Tony's a stand-up guy."

"Don't waste your time. I forgot him the moment I raced through a packed terminal, knocking over small children and little old ladies to catch my flight."

Ariel's familiar laugh filled the empty space in Sierra's car. "You didn't."

"If it wasn't for a low-cut top I wore for Tony's benefit, I would have missed the flight for sure. Lucky for me, I scored TSA pre-check and a flirtatious security agent who whisked me through the line."

"OMG, Sierra."

"All I can say is, don't expect me for future reunions if Tony is invited."

"I hope you realize I would have stepped in if I thought he might treat you this way."

"I'm not blaming *you*. My first clue should have been when he kidnapped the groom. Besides, every girl deserves the experience of being stood up once in her life. I've met my quota. I can now close this chapter and move on.

"Still, Gavin needs to have a *mano y mano* talk with Mr. Franco. You're my best friend and I'm pissed he disrespected you."

"I'll admit I was disappointed and angry, followed

by shaken up at the gall of his behavior but talking to you has put things in perspective. I'm cool and I'll be even cooler after a good night's sleep."

"Sounds like a plan. Lunch later this week at our favorite bistro?"

"Yummy and yes. Call me."

****

"Uh-hum."

Gavin glanced up from his desk and the stack of order forms requiring his signature.

Ariel placed herself in his direct line of vision and with her hands on her hips, shoulders back, she asked, "Honey, you got a sec?"

He didn't think for one second, he had a choice. He smiled and cocked an eyebrow, curious about what had riled his usually laid-back wife. "What's up, babe?"

"Tony stood up Sierra."

His face scrunched. "What?"

"In case you were too preoccupied at the wedding to notice," she said, exaggerating her words with a wink, "Tony pursued Sierra with a 'take no hostages attitude' until she said yes to dinner and then failed to show at the hotel where he promised to pick her up."

Gavin furrowed his brow and shook his head like a dog after a bath. "When did they start dating?"

Ariel, her fist closed, punched his bicep, "Don't be dense. She almost missed her flight."

"Damn woman, you're calling me names?" He grunted. "Why do I have the feeling Tony's lapse in judgment is somehow my fault?"

"So, he hasn't talked to you about Sierra?"

Gavin placed his hands over his eyes, then his ears and lastly, his mouth, in succession.

"You're incorrigible." Attempting a stern face, she stamped one foot. "While Sierra was in Los Angeles conducting a Zumba Master Class, they connected. He asked her to dinner and offered to drive her to the airport. Then he didn't bother to show and didn't even call to cancel. Does that sound like him?"

"No, it doesn't." He frowned and reached for his cell phone, "I'll call him," he said as he rolled back his chair. "Something you should know about Tony."

"What?"

"Like most SEALS, he has a past. One that drives him daily."

Ariel fisted her hand on her jutted hip. "What sort of past could drive him to be a thoughtless dick?"

"Whoa." Gavin held up his palm, facing her. "You don't have the facts. That's what I'm trying to tell you." His leg bounced up and down as he spoke. "Tony was the unpopular kid in school, so he routinely got beaten up by bullies on his way home. But he learned how to defeat a bigger, stronger enemy."

"I give…How?"

"He stopped taking the bus and ran from school, past the bus stop, all the way home. While driving the bullies nuts, Tony became a superb runner."

"I'm sorry he was beaten up but what does his past have to do with him standing up Sierra?"

"Tony is not an insensitive, shallow guy. He's a planner and a thinker. There has to be a good reason for him not showing."

Ariel closed her hand around Gavin's open palm and squeezed. "I believe you."

His groin tightened as her wide, doe eyes searched his face. "That's good," he said and flashed her a grin.

"Will you fill me in when you find out what happened, please?"

He grabbed her chin and planted a quick peck on her lips "Of course." Inches from her mouth, the subtle scent of butterscotch beckoned him to close the distance and suck the taste of it off her tongue.

As if she sensed the consequences of his desire, she retreated a step and kissed her index finger before placing it on his lips. "Would you call him now?"

Gavin groaned. "Yes, and I'll found out what happened from Franco."

"Thanks, and babe?" before he could respond, she continued, "no good deed goes unpunished." She smiled, lifted her T-shirt and flashed him her bra-filled bosom.

"Holy shit," he said before bolting toward the French doors, punching in numbers as he broke into a run for the backyard where he could hear Tony's lame excuses in private. He refused to allow his thoughts to dip into the dark well of more sinister possibilities. Then, he'd offer himself up for some good ole fashioned 'punishment.'

Chapter Ten

Sierra raised her voice over the chatty din as she tapped the green arrow on her tablet. "C'mon ladies. Time to get sexy."

The overhead clapping of hands accompanied the steady beat of the music as she cued the forty students dressed in tank tops and yoga pants to sidestep first to the left, then back to the right. She loved teaching Zumba. The Latin origin guaranteed a sensual embrace of fast-paced rhythms choreographed into hip-jiggling, shoulder-shimmying routines guaranteed to burn calories and pump out positive energy. Men also participated in Zumba, but they were the few, the proud and the brave, like Tony's uninhibited jumping in at the wedding reception. *No doubt about it, the man can dance. Crap. Focus Sierra.*

With her fingers stretching her lips into a mock smile, she encouraged the ladies to shut out, if for only an hour, the morning battle over getting the kids ready for school or disappointment of being passed over for a raise—or being stood up by an undeniably hot guy.

As the session warm-up continued, sweat blossomed on the temples of the dancing throng who echoed the 'whoop, whoop' of the current song. The students glided and swirled in unison, mirror-imaging their instructor's movements. She plunged into deep squats, arms flung forward with each downward shift.

"Booties in the air like you don't care, ladies," she called out with her signature enthusiasm while advancing into the front line of students and engaging them eye to eye. "How deep can you squat?" she challenged. They complied in giggling groans and mock moans.

With the warm-up completed, Sierra accelerated the pace of the routines until heads were drenched and modified tank tops clung damply to semi-bare backs. The mood transformed from anticipation to a chill, relaxed vibe as song after song played and built-up stress melted from each person's space. *I may not be saving the world from terrorists like Gavin and his buddies did, but I am gifting my class with a bit of temporary peace and joy.*

She darted for the stage after tapping her tablet for the next song "You are going to love this new choreo."

A Latin rhythm erupted from the speakers, sparking everyone into a unified Salsa step. Zumba represented diversity at its ever loving best. Fat women, skinny girls, senior ladies and young mothers moved together, enjoying each other's company. Race and socio-economics didn't matter. Politics never entered the mix.

"C'mon," she yelled and cued the next transition as she gazed out at the class with suppressed amusement at the different interpretations of dance. One didn't need to be a great dancer to Zumba, but a good sense of rhythm helped. If a man showed up for class, well, bonus time because Sierra considered him fair game for extra attention, much to the delight of the other women.

The subsequent song rolled into the final beats of the current tune. With her attention zeroed in on the one male student, she waved him on stage. The class cheered as he jumped on the platform.

"Woot, Woot," she responded as they danced together in mock flirtation.

Memories of her first encounter with Tony at the hospital pushed into her mind. He'd flirted—and she'd liked it despite the headache. Then the wedding day came and he turned into the headache. The reception equaled another flirt fest in a 'hate you, like you' kind of way. So, when he made the effort to hook up in LA, she took the bait. Big mistake.

Well, fool me once but it wouldn't be fool me twice. As the song ended, so did the flash from the past. "Don't forget to hydrate, ladies," she said before taking a swig from her own water bottle. "One more song, then cool down."

In more ways than one.

Chapter Eleven

"Answer the phone, Tony." After four unanswered rings, Gavin sought the shade of a large oak tree to minimize the sun's intensity.

"*You know the drill*," Tony's voice message played, followed by an annoying beep.

"Rrrgh. Damn it, man." Gavin slammed his fist into the tree. "Where are you?"

He tapped the end button and stared at the empty screen for a few seconds before scrolling through his contact list until it landed on Bill Evanston, fondly nicknamed Pudge, by his platoon mates.

SEALs were legendary for assigning disparaging nicknames to each other. Pudge was no exception. Gavin snorted at the memory of the baby fat around Evanston's middle jiggling when he ran. He couldn't remember who came up with the handle, but the best nicknames burrowed under the skin like a wood sliver and festered. This choice was spot-on and perhaps motivated him to achieve the status of one of the top runners in his BUDS class.

After selecting Pudge's mobile number, Gavin swiveled his neck to locate his omniscient wife who could decipher a brow twitch. He wasn't ready to alarm her with the wanted status of his closest friend. They were due to leave on their honeymoon next week and she was in full planning mode for their European river cruise. He'd been all over Europe while in the Navy and could care less. What he did care about was being wherever she was and making her happy.

"Hello?" Pudge answered.

"Is Tony with you?" Gavin barked.

"Asleep next to me."

"What the hell, Pudge. Where are you two?"

"In my car, speeding down I-10 toward Tucson. We're driving flat out. Be there in four days."

"Jesus. Is Tony in one piece?"

"Yeah, with a few cracks."

"What happened?"

"Not sure yet. I have a friend investigating the cause of the crash."

"Have him call me on the burner phone I hope he bought," Gavin snapped. "I want a full debrief."

"Done and will do.

****

"That about sums up the situation," Tony said as the car breezed by the *Welcome to El Paso* sign on I-10.

At Gavin's insistence, he'd recounted the highlights of his brakes failing and the resultant decision to move up the time line for leaving LA. Together they decided to include Ariel in the situation report. She understood the significance of a sit rep. Besides, it would get Gavin off the hook and off the proverbial sofa, but Gavin agreed she'd be sworn to secrecy. Best if the truth came directly from him to Sierra, in person.

Gavin heaved a heavy sigh, "I hope you guys brought your cold-weather gear."

"Huh?" Tony queried.

"After I tell my wife the necessity of postponing our honeymoon, Ocala's going to resemble the frozen

71

Alaskan Tundra for a few days."

"I'm sorry, man. I never wanted to involve you or put your family in harm's way."

"Strange words coming from someone who kidnapped me the night before my wedding."

Tony pictured Gavin's right eyebrow lift with a sardonic smile. "If it makes you feel any better, I'm most likely facing my own ice storm or more likely fire storm from Sierra when she finds out I'm within punching distance."

"Bottom line, we stand together. I'll call a few other Team guys. We'll meet in three days at the farm. Drive…safe," Gavin said and then hit end.

Chapter Twelve

On the fourth day of marathon driving, with the sun headed toward the western horizon, Tony veered off the paved country highway onto the gravel road to his best friend's horse farm in Ocala, Florida. He rubbed the scratchy scruff on his chin as he surveyed his new sanctuary from a truly messed up predicament.

His gut lurched at the thought of seeing Sierra-turned-hell cat and wondered if he could talk fast enough to avoid being verbally ripped to shreds. Dressed in cargo shorts, a T-shirt and open sandals for the long drive, he sneaked a quick sniff under his arms and regretted not showering and changing clothes before arriving.

As he steered the car around the circular drive to the front of the house, he noticed the porch swing rolling back and forth in a steady tilt by—uh oh—Sierra and Ariel. Bitter fluid rushed up his throat and he gripped the steering wheel as he pressed the brake pedal. "Wake up Pudge. I need reinforcements."

"Tough luck, buddy." Pudge chuckled as he surveyed the waiting pair. "All eyes on you."

Tony groaned as he jammed the gear shift into Park. "I'd rather soak in a barrel of hot pig grease than step out of this truck."

"I'll wait here while you test the waters."

"Chicken shit." Tony shouldered open the door and

got blasted by Florida's infamous heat and humidity.

Pudge exited from the passenger side in slow motion and edged to the rear of the truck. "I'll get the gear," he announced with a cheerful twang.

Tony shot him a disgusted glare before his gaze shifted from one woman to the other. Ariel stood and started toward him. Relieved, he focused his attention on her, knowing Gavin had relayed the situation. Her face bore no clue of whether he'd be welcomed with a hug or a verbal whiplash for hurting Sierra. His gut took another somersault.

She opened her arms in a welcoming gesture, a Mona Lisa smile crossing her lips. The warmth of her greeting relieved his anxiety. He blew out the breath he'd been holding with a heavy sigh and readied himself for her embrace.

Ariel wrapped her arms around his neck, and leaning in close to his ear, whispered, "Gavin swore me to secrecy. Sierra's been told nothing but you are in hot, deeply hot water, buddy."

Tony hugged her back while he glanced at the dark-haired beauty still glued to the seat of the swing. "If looks could kill," he replied, keeping his voice low, "there'd be a thousand daggers stuck in my chest." He released his grip on Ariel, nodded and smiled as if their conversation had been about the weather. "Thanks for the warning and sorry about the honeymoon."

"You're such a buzz kill, T-man," she said, leveling a mock punch to his shoulder. "I'll give you two some privacy." She veered off to the side of the house and disappeared.

Sierra stood, stick-straight, arms rigid at her side when Tony, hands in his pockets, strolled with a casual pace in her direction. "Hi," he said, wariness in his voice, as he climbed, weak-kneed onto the porch.

Without warning, she charged him and slammed her fist into his sternum. "You could have called."

"Ouch." He winced and clutched his chest. "I'm sorry. I would've if I could've."

"Sorry, doesn't cut it." She clenched her jaw and forcefully crossed her arms. "I almost missed my flight. And what do you mean, could have?"

"I was in an accident and was knocked out cold."

She arched a brow. "What kind of accident?"

"The intentional kind."

He waited expectantly for the realization he knew would occur. It took less than ten seconds until understanding blossomed across her face. Sierra's mouth gaped opened, but no words passed her lips. She jammed her hands on her hips. "Elaborate please."

"I can't. Only know the more I tell you, the greater the danger for you."

She persisted. "What kind of danger?"

"The kind I don't want you involved in."

"Enough talking in circles," she said, then added after several seconds, "maybe I can help. I've known danger before."

His thoughts raced. He didn't want to involve anyone else, most of all a civilian who doubtless lacked any defensive skills. She claimed to know danger, but he doubted she had familiarity with this much potential for violence. He weighed dragging her into the fray against the niggling desire to spend time with her. The idea of Sierra next to him, naked, tempted him beyond reason, clouding his judgment. Besides, they were safe here on the farm. For now.

His jaw clenched with determination. "Oh, you can help. Have dinner with me."

"Not a chance."

"C'mon, Sierra. Here on the farm. Tonight."

"Can you blame me for being somewhat skeptical after all the shenanigans you've pulled?

"Not at all. Listen." He shifted closer to place his hands on her shoulders. "If I hadn't been knocked out cold, I would've met you at the restaurant. I wanted to be there."

She didn't jerk away but her muscles twitched under his touch.

"We'll keep it informal. How about conversation and Italian pasta by the swimming pool?" Her shoulders relaxed, so he added, "After sundown, the weather is kind of perfect this time of year."

"Can you cook?"

"Are you kidding? I'm Italian. Wait 'til you taste my sausage and meatball spaghetti." He screwed his index finger into his dimple. "*Delizioso.*"

"Sounds tempting." Sierra duplicated Tony's hand gesture. "And heavy. And fattening."

He wanted to tell her she didn't need to worry about calories, and from his view, her body could stop traffic. Instead, he treaded carefully. "We swim after we eat. Work off the calories."

"You're such a charmer," she scoffed. "I'll agree to dinner, but on one condition."

"Name it."

"If you tell me what is going on, right now, full disclosure. And the swim's still a maybe."

Tony realized the uselessness of avoiding her ultimatum and, in total truth, he wanted to spend time with her. He sucked in a deep breath and blurted, "I have a bounty on my head, and I'm being hunted by ISIS assassins.

****

She threw her head back and laughed so hard, she snorted out her nose. "No way. Oh man." Her shoulders shook as she tried to suppress the giggles. "Really?"

"Way and man and really." They've already crossed the border from Mexico." He pressed his lips into a thin line.

Her mood changed from levity to disbelief to shocked surprise. "How did you find out?"

"I can't divulge that but let's say it wasn't on social media or the Internet."

"What did you do?"

"Can't talk about the specifics of the op. They're top secret. This is no joke."

She clasped her hands on either side of her head and then crossed herself. "Holy Mother of Mary."

****

"Hey, guys," Ariel called out through the screen door. "It's six o'clock. Time for dinner." She poked her head out. "We're going into town for supplies and a pizza. Interested?"

Sierra, although famished, decided Tony handed her the perfect opportunity to explore his complexities. Who knew the man had a serious side? He also cleaned up nicely and wow, after a shower, he smelled good. "Thanks. We're staying here."

Tony offered two thumbs in agreement and grabbed Sierra's hand. "Come with me."

She waved goodbye to the group as he tugged her backward toward a grassy slope behind the barn.

"Aren't you tired from your drive?" she asked, curious how two guys condensed a week's worth of driving into three days.

"Yeah, but I'm used to functioning on minimal sleep. Remember, I was a SEAL and now I work in an E.R." When he grinned, his demeanor changed to boyish and almost shy. "Besides, this is my chance to make things right."

She didn't remove her hand from his grip. Despite the earlier mishap, which resulted in her thinking he was a real dirt bag, she now understood the fun-loving daredevil had a valid reason for failing to pick her up. A sense of urgency possessed her. How much time did they have before all hell broke loose?

He pointed to a lush emerald hillside under an ancient oak tree and holding onto her hand, pulled her to the top where he indicated they should sit. He steadied her, while she plopped on the grass.

"Thanks." She gazed up into his intense, dark eyes. "I've been to this spot before with Ariel. We come here to talk when we need peace and solitude from the daily grind. Perfect spot for you to tell me the whole story." She patted the space next to her.

Tony sat and plucked a nearby blade of grass, sticking the long stem in his mouth. He leaned back, propped himself on his elbows and studied the sky. His quiet contemplation, she guessed, was his decision-making process and she was fine with the silence. After a full ten minutes, he sat upright and with the green stalk bobbing up and down, recounted the most bizarre tale she'd ever heard. Details were missing from the original mission that started the events rolling, but she didn't press him.

"What next?" she asked, satisfied a break-in, car crash and concussion were acceptable reasons for being stood up.

"This."

He rolled over and leaned in, his brown eyes smoldered as they focused on her lips. He kissed her, slow and gentle at first, but as she relented, he increased the pressure. The heat from his body simmered against her. She wrapped her arms around his neck, curling her fingers in his thick hair. He snuggled her closer before relaxing them both into a reclined position. Eyes closed, she curved her body into his, fitting her petite frame along his torso. He rolled on top, stretching her toned arms above her head. With access to her neck, he wasted no time burying his face in the crook, nuzzling and nipping the exposed flesh. She moaned and raised her hips in invitation.

He responded and rubbed his full erection between her legs. Senseless with desire, her heart thumped against her rib cage and her hardened nipples ached. Wanting more, she transferred Tony's hands from hers, and placed them on her breasts. With experienced skill, he massaged and squeezed her bosoms through her blouse, until she wanted nothing between his touch and her skin.

Driven by a raw and uncontrolled passion she tugged at the buttons of her shirt. The thought of ripping them off crossed her mind. Anticipation of him rolling her hard, bare nipple between his fingertips had her panting when a hot breath blew on her face. She opened her eyes to a whisker-covered muzzle curiously inspecting the top of Tony's head.

"Oh crap!"

"What the hell?" He rolled onto his knees, and whipped his head around, fists clenched close to his chest, but when he comprehended the source of Sierra's startled squeal, he relaxed and pushed himself to his feet next to her.

The horse reacted to the commotion by tossing his head as he curled his upper lip.

"Is he laughing at us?" she asked him.

"No, but if I was him, I would be." Tony smiled and eased his junk in a more comfortable position. "Git." He waved his arm at the four-legged intruder who blinked placidly back but didn't budge. "Shoo, now."

"Shoo?" She giggled. "You're going to command a two-thousand-pound beast with 'shoo'?"

He opened his mouth, she guessed, in defense of his word choice but most likely realized how ridiculous he sounded, even to the horse. Instead, he offered a few firm slaps to the equine's neck. The horse simply tossed his head in apparent satisfaction and trotted off down the hill. Sierra giggled and straightened her blouse. "That horse is such a spoilsport."

Tony waggled both brows. "Would some good Italian pasta, the food of love, help reignite your appetite?"

Not missing the innuendo, she said, "I'll race you to the kitchen." She didn't wait for Tony's agreement and charged down the hill, confident he couldn't catch her and would remain in her laughter's wake.

****

Tony peered over Sierra's shoulder as she used a wooden spoon and fork to mix fresh vegetables. "You toss a mean salad."

"You run a mean race," she countered.

"What are you talking about? You beat me."

"You let me win." She smacked him on his arm with the spoon. "Don't try to deny it."

He lifted his shoulders and showed her his palms. *Yes, I let you win but it was worth restraining myself to see you happy and not pissed at me anymore. And then there was also watching your cute little ass jiggle down the hill.*

"Salad looks great," he said, changing the subject as he side-stepped to the stove.

"A few tomatoes, a radish or two, some lettuce and chopped celery. How hard could it be?"

Holding a wooden spoon, and with his head bowed to test the marinara sauce he'd prepared, he mumbled, "Oh, it could be pretty hard."

Grinning, she stuck her finger in the sauce, licked it off and snickered. "You're incorrigible."

"I try." He grinned. "We're ready here," he smacked his lips. "The sauce is done. I'll grab a tray and we can eat by the pool."

She held the door as he slipped through with the food bowls stacked precariously on the tray. "I'll grab some wine and my portable music. The outdoor speaker system is top of the line. What music genre do you prefer?"

He inhaled the lavender scent wafting off her hair as he slid next to her in the tight space."Hard rock."

Her eyes widened. "Uh.... okay. Not music I'd normally dance to. More like head banging. I was thinking Latin Salsa or Enrique style tunes."

"Who said anything about dancing?"

"I thought it would be fun after we eat."

"Sure, if you're talking about mattress dancing."

She exaggerated an eye roll. "Okay, schoolboy."

He laughed at her dig. "We could compromise with alternative."

"Hmmm. I love alternative and a lot of the music is danceable. Besides, music of any kind with wine is always a good combination. By the way, what kind of wine do you prefer?"

Tony flicked the lighter and held it over one of the candles on the wrought iron table. "Beer." He lifted his head and grinned. "Accompanied by candlelight."

"That does it. I'm picking the wine and the music."

As she bee-lined back to the house to retrieve her music and he hoped, a bottle of Riesling, he noticed her shoulders jiggling with laughter over their banter. *I could almost forget the danger I'm in but it's coming, and I don't want her near me when it crashes down.*

The pool lights, which he'd flicked on earlier, rotated in a rainbow of colors. "Perfect."

With his head tilted skyward, he inhaled the fresh country air tinged with the scent of orange blossoms. The light from the full moon and stars cast an ethereal glow over the nearby woods. He scanned the surrounding landscape but perceived nothing unusual. The nondescript, nylon pouch draped across the back of his chair held his 9mm, just in case. He wasn't certain how Sierra viewed guns, but his weapon was like a third arm, and vital at times like this. If she had any concerns, he'd have to deal.

His stomach growled, distracting him as he mused, "Italian pasta wasn't the only thing he was craving."

Sierra's hips swayed back and forth as she increased the volume on the state-of-the-art stereo system. Melodic Spanish lyrics swept in waves across the open space.

He called out, "Chow's ready." Then pointed to the speakers, and in a teasing tone said, "Great choice."

She danced toward him with a playful flip of her dark hair and shimmied her shoulders as she crossed one foot in front of the other. He pulled out her chair and with a graceful swoop of his hand, indicated she should sit. She swerved onto the seat and smiled as he draped the napkin across her lap.

"Dig in," he said, pointing to the bowl of pasta and slid into his seat.

"Smells yummy." She heaped a pile of noodles onto her plate, stuck her fork through a few tubes of cooked pasta and plopped them in her mouth. She closed her eyes and licked her lips. "Ummm…. Divine, Chef Tony."

"I'll say," he muttered, his attention focused on the constant, slight up-curve of her lips.

She blushed and dotted her napkin with delicate pats around the corners of her mouth. "How or maybe why, I should ask, did you became a SEAL?"

Tony hesitated, and then took a sip of the semi-sweet Riesling she'd chosen. He peered over the top of the glass, watched as Sierra shoveled more food into what seemed like a bottomless pit. Not one ounce of excess fat on her body, but the woman could eat.

"The why was 9/11. The how?" He grunted. "I grew up on the streets and alleys of Santa Monica, California, unmonitored by hippie parents who never bothered to get married." *Man, I sound bitter.* "My childhood was okay. I wasn't abused, and my Dad taught me to surf…right before he took off. My mother did her best to raise me, but motherhood wasn't her forte. Neither was marriage." He took a deep gulp of wine and set the glass on the table. "She's on her third husband who is a reasonably nice guy."

"Do you have a relationship with her?"

"Yes. She lives in Northern California, only about eight hours from LA. I drive up when I can and we have lunch."

"What about your dad? Did you ever see him again after he left?"

Tony propped his elbows on the table and steepled his hands under his chin. "My mother's second husband turned out to be a son-of-a-bitch who didn't want me around. When she found a birthday card my dad sent me, complete with a return address, she contacted him and asked, probably begged, him to take me. She concluded I'd be better off with my father than her butt-head husband."

Sierra's eyes widened. "Why didn't she just leave the guy?"

"We didn't have much money. She had no skills and couldn't find sustainable employment. In her defense, I think she believed her new husband would provide for both of us."

"Did you go live with your dad?"

He nodded. "Right after my thirteenth birthday, I moved to Texas where he'd relocated and lived with him until he died of AIDS."

Sierra put her fork down. "Tony, what a tough way to grow up."

He shrugged. "The worst part was my father came from a wealthy, society family who had a reputation to protect. They never accepted or even acknowledged my existence. After high school, I opted to enlist in the military. The recruiter convinced me the Navy was my best option and in the back of my mind I wanted to see if I had what it took to become a SEAL. But the plan got waylaid when I was offered a lacrosse scholarship from Syracuse University. I figured after graduation, I'd join up as an officer and make it a career."

"Was there a pivotal moment when you decided to quit school and enlist?"

"Right after 9/11." He paused. "Combined with my girlfriend dumping me after she found out I signed up." He scoffed. "Her definition of success didn't include an enlisted Navy puke. She wanted me to finish college."

"Wait a minute." She touched his arm. "A puke?"

A smile broke across his tense face. "That's how we enlisted guys assume officers, who we call zipper heads, view us."

Sierra fake-coughed and shook her head in apparent amusement. With the added levity, Tony relaxed and sipped another taste of wine. "I had no one to worry about and nothing to lose so I took the tests required to join the military and scored high enough to do the physical try out for the Teams."

"Which you passed with flying colors?"

"I was a skinny but athletic kid and lacrosse built me up physically."

"Any regrets?"

"Not even one." He cleared his throat. "The Team is my family now. The one I never had growing up."

Sierra lowered her outstretched hand to the table. "I get it. Thanks for sharing."

Tony grasped her fingertips, "Satisfied?"

"Yes, in more ways than one. You certainly can

cook. I'm stuffed."

"Very tactical change of subject and you're welcome. Rigatoni with sausages is the only dish I can cook." He laughed; his mood lightened in great measure by her obvious acceptance of his past.

"Your turn."

"Nothing much to say." She shrugged. "I was born in a small mountain village in Colombia, South America. My father relocated to Caquetá to teach high school where he met my mother, an American who worked for the USAID." Something about the name of the city jarred a memory from Tony's military years and he made a mental note to Google the location.

"After my mother died," she said with a noticeably hard swallow, "my father was devastated and never fully recovered from the loss. I was too young to fend for myself so his brother, my uncle Alex who owned and operated a circus, encouraged me to relocate to the United States when I was a teenager. He raised me and paid for my college education and law school.

Sierra shoved back her chair and stood, scooping up her dinner plate. As she reached for his dinnerware, he grabbed her hand and hauled her into his lap. "Let me go," she squealed. You cooked. I'll clean up."

He noticed her palms were sweaty and had a gut feeling she'd only skimmed over the telling of her past. Law school was a big deal but she'd never mentioned it before now. "You have a law degree?"

With her bright green eyes leveled at his face, she huffed, "Is being an attorney so hard to believe?"

"No." He took the plate from her and placed it on the table. His throat tightened, making it hard to swallow or speak, "Leave it." He laced his fingers into her glossy, brunette hair, wrapped the curly strands around his hand and tugged her face so their noses touched. "Not at all but if you don't mind me asking, why aren't you practicing law?"

"I still need to take the bar."

"Don't most people do that soon after graduation?"

"Most do. I chose to get certified as a Zumba instructor first."

"Why do I feel there is more to this story than you're telling?"

She squirmed in his lap. "Because there is. My father died while I was in my final semester of law school and I couldn't fly back to Colombia to attend the funeral. In fact, I wasn't able to correspond with him much at all after I moved here."

He tried to put together the time line of her past few years. Something didn't fit.

She continued. "I'm studying to take the bar next February but even after I pass it, I'll never give up teaching Zumba. The community is so supportive, and the positive energy is therapeutic."

What was she hiding? His gut told him if he pushed any harder, he'd blow the mood.

He placed his index finger across her lips. "We all have a past. I was a decorated Navy SEAL who left a promising career to become a nurse practitioner and work in one of the busiest trauma units in the country. Blood and guts are not therapeutic or uplifting but helping the poor souls who lie bleeding to death on an exam table is something I'm good at."

She flattened her palm on his chest. "One day when we haven't had such a satisfying meal and I'm not dying to work off a few calories, I'll answer all your questions. Deal?"

"Deal. Want to dance, Miss Attorney?"

The current song was a slow, love ballad. "Sure." She pressed her hands down on his thighs to lever herself to a standing position. "We could dance a little Salsa?"

"Salsa?"

"C'mon. Don't pretend it's a foreign concept. I saw you dancing at the wedding."

Tony leaped up and hugged her tight to his chest, soaking in the softness of her cheek nestled against his stubble. "Not what I had in mind."

They danced in a two-foot radius and were both breathing hard as they swayed to the sensuous rhythm. Tony noticed Sierra's pulse jump in her throat and tugged her tighter to his chest. He leaned back and peered into the deep emerald pools of her eyes. His hand fell to her bottom and gripped her ample cheek, hugged her to his crotch and his growing erection.

She sighed and followed his lead as he continued guiding her around the paved adobe deck. He snaked his hand between the slim space of their bodies and began a circular massage of her breast. She gasped and palmed Tony in the chest, thrusting him onto the poolside edge. Surprised and off balance his arms wind-milled backwards as his groin arched forward. Sierra grabbed the waist of his shorts, but gravity prevailed and like dominoes they toppled into the water.

When she bobbed to the surface, he was waiting for her, laughing and spitting out water. "Want to go swimming?"

"I don't have a suit with me, and these clothes are waterlogged," she said as she half swam, half walked to the side of the pool.

In one lithe motion, he vaulted out of the pool. "So what's the problem?"

****

Speechless, she gawked as he peeled his T-shirt over his head and dropped his camouflage shorts, all commando, as if he was in a men's locker room. *No boxers or briefs?*

Except in a men's locker room she doubted he'd have an erection. Don't stare, she told herself, but her gaze stayed glued on his boner. Eyes up, she commanded but they didn't comply.

"Oh, what the heck," she mumbled and unbuttoned her blouse, tossing it on the pool deck. Next, she tugged off her capri pants, swirled them in the air and aimed or the chaise lounge. "Missed. Ugh."

An approving smile crept across Tony's face as she unhooked her bra and flung it to the ground. The chill in the night air stiffened her nipples. He held out his hand and she twined her fingers with his. His gaze drifted to her panties with a raised eyebrow. She shrugged and balanced on one foot, then the other as she slid the lacy undergarment down her legs.

"Calorie burn time," she said, stepping to the edge of the Olympic sized pool.

Tony edged up beside her. "What'd you have in mind?"

"Aqua Zumba," she called over her shoulder as she jumped in feet first.

"What the hell." He plunged in behind her with a wave- making cannonball.

The water, warmed from the intense Florida sun, offered a sensuous gift against her naked skin. Sierra leaned back against the cement side and gazed up at the star-filled night as she kicked her legs in a graceful rhythm, toes pointed, up and down, up and down. She couldn't remember a time she'd felt so comfortable or safe with a man. He was a loner but had opened to her in a way she doubted he did ever, if at all.

Tony glided through the water in a smooth breaststroke like a heat seeking missile. His muscles flexed as he braced an arm on either side of her. *No escape. Not that I want one.* Sierra gazed into his eyes, sparking with desire and intertwined her legs with his. She'd made her decision. She wouldn't resist his advance. Her chest tight, she heaved a sigh as she succumbed to the overwhelming need to have him fill her. She wrapped her arms around his thick neck and her legs around his waist. He leaned forward; head tilted to the side, and kissed her, a slow, soft kiss. He drew back and gazed into her eyes, gauging her reaction. "I want this to be right."

With those few words her barriers shattered. Heat and need spread like wildfire engulfing her body. She pierced his mouth with her tongue in a wild and frantic dance. He welcomed her onslaught with a guttural moan. With her legs around his firm, rounded ass, she tugged him to her moist center. Without unlocking their lips, Tony slid his penis back and forth between the top of her thighs in a slow rhythmic motion.

"Ahhh…" Her head fell back; she bucked against him. "More. Give me more."

Tony grabbed her hand and tugged her to the stairs. "The recliners…more comfortable," he stuttered, then nodded toward the double lounger. She fell limp against his chest as he scooped her into his arms and carried her out of the water. He kept eye contact as he laid her on the cushion and hovered over her naked body.

Wrapping her arms around his neck she arched her back and proffered her breast to his mouth. He dipped his head and feasted on her nipples, relentless in his sucking and tugging as he lowered his torso until the hair on his chest rubbed against her soft, smooth skin. He pressed against her opening and groaned. Unable to withstand the intense throbbing another second, she reached between his legs and guided him into her.

The penetration was heaven. She gasped as he thrust deeper. He was better endowed than most men she'd been with. On his next thrust he sucked her breast into his mouth and nibbled on her nipple. Her desire roared. The pounding in her chest was matched only by the throbbing between her legs. She exploded with carnal desire; her hedonistic scream ignited the still summer air. Tony responded to her cry of pleasure with a final deep thrust sending his release exploding inside her. His shoulders slumped as the taut muscles in his back and arms relaxed. He dropped tender kisses in the crook of her neck before he eased his body to her side. "You're so beautiful, Sierra."

"You're kind of smoking hot, yourself," she replied, bumping her fist off his shoulder and hoping she sounded casual because the lingering, full body tingle had her doubting her own sanity.

"I wanted you the first time I saw you." His soulful, penetrating stare raised goosebumps on her arms. "And I care about you." He massaged his foot along her leg.

"Honestly, I care about you too but escaping the bounty on your head should be your top priority."

"You're right but I don't want to leave you."

"I don't want you to go either but I'd rather have you alive and somewhere safe, than dead." She hung her head, eyes focused on the pebbled cement below the chair.

"Dead?" He winked and lifted her chin to eye level. "Not a chance."

Chapter Thirteen

Awakened by the deep rumbling of male voices, Sierra, eyes still closed, flung her arm over the side of the bed and probed for the boy shorts and T-shirt Tony had stripped off her last night. Unable to convince her to sleep in his room, the early morning hours provided cover for him to slip into hers. Call it modesty or discretion, but she wasn't ready to make their budding relationship a "family" affair. Too many questions would be asked by the people downstairs.

Her hand connected with the soft material. *Umm. Here they are.* Opening her eyelids in a squint, she pulled on the pants and then sat up to tug the top over her head. Wondering if the mind-numbing level of satisfaction might show in her expression, she entered the *en suite* bathroom and stared in the mirror, turning her face side to side.

Nope. My secret's safe-unless they heard us. Oh, geez, Sierra, don't go there.

One of Ariel's silky robes hung on a wall hook, so she slipped it on and after combing her fingers through her unruly curls, proceeded down the stairs.

The voices, along with the smell of frying bacon, drew her to the kitchen. Pausing in the entryway, she realized Tony's attention was fixed on the doorway and her. With a heated gaze his eyes surveyed her body up and down before asking, "Did we wake you?"

A shiver cascaded down her arms, on instinct she tugged the robe belt tighter. "To be honest, yes, but I'm an early riser so no worries." She responded in the same casual tone he'd used.

Tony smiled and nodded toward the counter. "Coffee's ready."

Ariel poured a cup and added cream and sugar before handing it to her. "Your favorite mug," she said with a giggle. The gold script across the front read, "Queen of Fucking Everything."

Sierra smiled broadly, then sipped a taste as she peeked over the top of the rim at her best friend. *Did she know?* Suddenly, the quote seemed like innuendo instead of a tease about her full tilt approach for life. She decided it didn't matter. When the time was right, she'd share all the ways Tony made her feel like a queen.

Ariel topped off their mugs and both women directed their attention to the men who were hunkered down, speaking in hushed voices while they inspected maps of the property. Soldier of Fortune magazine could not have staged a more perfect cover. Three specimens of male perfection assembled around an oak breakfast table complete with morning scruff and angular features. They sipped their brew with intense concentration as each man voiced his opinion.

Dressed in the same light brown T-shirts over tan camouflaged pants, each wore a thigh holster loaded with what Sierra assumed was a well-broken-in gun. Tony was the exception, in jeans and a T-shirt but no apparent gun—unless it was tucked in the waistband at the small of his back.

She leaned against the marble counter while her

mind wandered into a dark past. A time she'd forced into the recesses of her mind and with very real purpose had tried to forget. The experience had been life altering and involved capture by a paramilitary group, terrorists really, in her native country. Her captivity had lasted a year. During that time, she'd slept with one eye open, hoping the leader's obvious fascination with her would keep her alive as well as prevent rape by other group members. Escape was impossible in the jungles of Putumayo, so she prayed daily for rescue. When that day finally came, the battle turned bloody. Under a blur of bullets, she was thrown over a soldier's shoulder and carried out to safety.

With a deliberate shake of her head and shoulders, Sierra purposely stopped the resurgence of ugly memories and forced her attention to the present.

Surveying the comradery of the men around the table, she realized her ingrained suspicion of tough, alpha men was skewed. These guys were different, with her best friend's husband topping the list of different. She'd never met a more honorable person. Service to God and country: a common bond among these men.

Gavin had a pad of paper in front of him. "We have to get our asses in gear and develop a strategy."

Pudge added, "I spoke to my friend last night and he discovered vise grips on your car's brake line, Tony. Very difficult to spot on a cursory check. These bastards are devious and don't want to be discovered by simply blowing up your car with you in it. They most likely need proof of death to collect the bounty which means having you in one recognizable piece."

"Persistent," Gavin said. "Devious and persistent. We need to develop a contingency plan."

"I may have bought us some time," Pudge said. "I'd bet good money these bad actors are on their way to Iowa."

A partial frown creased Tony's brow. "Why?"

"As we installed surveillance equipment in your apartment, I slipped a couple brochures for Iowa in your dresser drawer, and highlighted a certain address in your little black book. Did you know your favorite uncle runs a pig farm outside of Altoona? Misdirection will give them something to chew on and buy us time."

Tony's robust laugh filled the crowded space and his shoulders shook vigorously. "Sidetracked to the heartland of America could have them questioning their dedication to whacking me."

"Would someone clue me in?" Sierra's outburst into the conversation drew everyone's attention. With all eyes on her, she slid behind Tony's chair and anchored her palms to the top rails of his chair in a white-knuckled grip.

Void of any emotion in his voice, he tilted his head and said, "I have to go into hiding…away from here…for a short time…until we have a plan in place and the threat can be ID'd and eradicated."

Out of nowhere, an idea struck. She swallowed the lump developing in her throat but went on. "I have an idea. It's a little off the radar but a member of my family owns a circus…."

Pudge interrupted with a chuckle. "We could dress Tony up in a clown costume. Oh wait, that won't work. Everyone would still recognize him."

Suddenly, Pudge's chair pitched backward in a free fall. Sierra gasped as Gavin, with lightning reflexes, caught the top slat mere inches from the floor. "Play nice, boys," he growled as he righted the chair with Pudge clutching both sides for balance.

As if he'd not just kicked Pudge's chair backward with the force of a mule, Tony glanced at Sierra. "What is your idea, sweetheart?"

Edging to his side, she said hesitantly, "My uncle owns and operates a circus. They've been wintering in Sarasota but will begin the northern circuit in a few days. A convoy of eighteen wheelers would be a great cover for a safe house, don't you think?"

Ariel asked, "Wouldn't a new arrival, someone with the superb physical conditioning of a SEAL, for instance, stand out in a circus family?"

"Not if he joined as a horse trainer," Tony said.

"How do you know about horses?" Sierra asked.

"I spent my summers on a ranch…with my father." His jaw twitched as he studied his hands. "He was a horse trainer by profession. I shadowed him and learned the ropes."

"I like it," Gavin said. "It would allow us time to track down these guys." He crooked his head to face Sierra. "No offense but can we trust your uncle?"

"None taken. My uncle took me in after my mother…um…died," she looked away, took a deep breath then turned toward Gavin. "He raised me with love and a strong work ethic. He supported me through college and all he's ever asked in return is for me to appreciate this country and the opportunities that living here provides."

Gavin said, "Guys, I think we have a winner."

All heads nodded in agreement.

"Shouldn't you notify the FBI?" Sierra asked. "Or at least the local sheriff?"

Suddenly a heavy curtain dropped over the room. Lighthearted teasing and macho jibes went dark with unspoken communications as the men transferred their thoughts via rapid head bobs and darting eyes.

"Hmm." She gave Ariel a nod. "Must be the hidden language of SEALS."

"I've notified a friend in the sheriff's office," Gavin said. "When the time is right, he'll assist. First, we need to establish Tony's cover, then confirm location of the tangos. I doubt the FBI has these guys on their radar since they're not your typical terrorist seeking mass destruction."

"Just *my* destruction," Tony scoffed.

Sierra squeezed his shoulders, then turned to find the nearest phone. "I'll contact my uncle and make the arrangements."

He caught her arm as she passed him, "Thanks."

"No problem." She shifted her gaze to the bulging muscle in his forearm, and had a brief memory of the night past. "I need to get going."

He slid his hand to hers and squeezed before letting go. "Where're you headed?"

"I teach a children's Zumba class once a week."

Tony caressed her wrist with feather strokes and gazed into the brilliant green of her eyes. "Want some company?"

"Huh?"

He pointed to his chest and then to her. "Me, you, together. *Capisce*?"

"I don't know what to say. Aren't you supposed to shelter in place? Plus, I didn't realize you like kids."

He raised his eyebrows and smiled. "Is that a yes?"

"No comments on my teaching techniques."

"No problem. You're driving so if I misbehave, you can make me thumb my way back here."

She swiped at his well-defined chest. "Not that I could make you do anything."

With a laugh, he dodged her hand. "Humble and kind. That's me."

****

Tony entered the kitchen, now vacated by the other men, with a large gym bag slung over his shoulder. He tugged his baseball cap low over his face and straightened his sunglasses before asking, "Ready?"

Sierra's mouth gaped open at first glance. "You're almost unrecognizable."

"That's the point."

She rubbed her knuckles over his growing stubble. "I like the facial hair."

Tony drew her hand to his mouth and kissed her knuckles. "I'm glad."

"I called my uncle while you were changing."

"How much did you tell him?"

"Enough." She shoved a piece of paper into his hand. "He said to give you his private cell number. Do you think the bad guys are already here in Florida?"

"No, I don't but never underestimate the enemy. These guys are not the barbarians you read about in the newspaper. They have an advanced intelligence network and plenty of allies here in the U.S. to help them with weapons, surveillance, computer hacking and financial aid, among other things."

"You're starting to scare me, Tony."

He matched her intense stare as he drew her close. "I want to protect you and the best way is by disguising my appearance and making myself scarce."

Still held in his tight embrace, she leaned back and fingered his sideburns. "Not sure how I feel about the blonde makeover."

Tony flipped the cap off his forehead and gave the wig a tug. "Temporary hair. Like the beard. No biggie."

She batted her eyelashes and slid the hat forward over his brow. "This kind of feels naughty like I'm in the arms of another man."

He grabbed the newspaper off the counter and with his finger pointing toward the headlines, said, "Horny Zumba instructor found in the arms of—" He grinned. "—her disguised but grateful boyfriend."

Sierra's stomach flipped at his issued designation of being her boyfriend. The more time she spent with this man the more time she wanted to spend with him but at what risk? The few former lovers she'd had included a hockey player, another Zumba instructor and oh yeah, an accountant. Hardly members of the gun-toting warrior breed. Today, he appeared like any guy going to the gym in his Oakley T-shirt, running shorts and laced up tennis shoes. "You have water in your overstuffed gym bag?"

Tony peered sideways into the bag and grinned. "Water, check. Towel, check. Pistol and extra magazines loaded with ammo, check."

"For Pete's sake. This is a children's class. Is it necessary to bring a loaded weapon?"

Tony's nostrils flared; his dark eyes flashed momentarily. "You're right. There's a circle of danger around me and anyone included in the circle is at risk. Better if I stay away from you for the time being." He released his grip on the bag, allowing it to drop on the table with a thud. "Better get going. You'll be late."

Sierra folded her arms. "No, I totally want you to go. Can we compromise?"

"How?"

"Will you leave your gun in the car?"

He rolled his eyes. "That'll help if my 'fan club' shows up because you can bet your sweet ass they'll be locked and loaded."

"I see your point." Sierra chewed on her lower lip and pleaded with her eyes. "But they're only children."

Tony concentrated on her face for a moment, then with delicate pressure, outlined her mouth with his finger, forcing her to relax her bite on her lip. "I'll risk it. For you. This once. Odds are those bozos are still in Iowa."

Chapter Fourteen

The parking lot was empty when they arrived at the studio. *Perfect*. He'd be able to study any new arrivals from his spot in the car, then check them out before they entered the building. Plus, he'd be armed.

Sierra hopped out and swung her bag over her shoulder. "Are you coming?"

"Go ahead and greet your students. I have a few phone calls to make."

"It's only a thirty-minute class." When he didn't offer an excuse, she shrugged and pressed her lips into a thin smile before tossing him the car keys and disappearing inside the dance studio.

Tony moved to the driver's seat and restarted the engine, then backed the car around into a face-out position. He punched in a familiar number.

Ariel picked up after one ring. "Tony. What's up?"

"I need a favor which involves you keeping a secret from Sierra." He didn't hear an end-the-call click; instead there was a deafening silence for a full five seconds on the other end.

"What else is new?" she asked on a throaty laugh.

Understanding her reasons for doubting his motives, he ignored the cynicism. "I would like your help finding a kitten for Sierra." The image of a solid gray, green eyed little purr factory stuck in his mind. "I'm going to be leaving soon and I don't want her to be lonely."

Ariel burst out laughing. "How do you know she even likes cats? Maybe she's a dog person."

"I figured a dog isn't practical because she travels but cats are so independent, kind of like her, and I, well…does she like cats?"

"Loves them," Ariel exclaimed. "But I have a feeling the kitten is more for you than for her. You want her to remember you every time she cuddles him or her. Am I correct?"

"Busted. Will you help me?"

"As a matter of fact, I spotted a notice on the bulletin board at the University of Florida a few days ago about free kittens. I'll call them after we hang up."

"Thanks. Pudge is in on this caper. Give him the kitten for safe keeping until I'm ready to ship out. I have another surprise for Sierra after her class today."

"Be careful, Franco. I don't want her safety compromised while tooling around with a hunted man."

"Heard, understood and acknowledged, ma'am. My own mother, bless her heart, wouldn't recognize me with my current disguise. I found a very secure hotel in Orlando with keyed entry elevators and rooms. I'm taking her there for the weekend. Pudge is briefed and has a lock on where I'm staying."

"Sounds like you've thought of everything. I'm less worried. Stand by. I'll get back to you about the kitten, either way."

After ten minutes, the last parent drove out of the parking lot for their normal routine of chatting over a cup of hipster brand coffee while their kids learned to Salsa. He shoved open the car door, resting one foot on the ground, then hesitated. The idea of being unarmed made him queasy.

The hair on the back of his neck stiffened. His backpack and its contents needed to remain in his possession. He promised Sierra he'd leave his weapon behind but wasn't her safety more important? Tony unzipped the top compartment of the backpack and removed a pair of long cargo pants; much easier to hide a gun in these pants than in running shorts, he thought. With a quick, visual inspection confirming the empty parking lot, he jumped out, and opened both the front and back doors, using them for privacy. He yanked the cloth down his legs and over his shoes and tugged the pants up over his bare butt. Satisfied with his decision, he retrieved his 9mm, winced when he stuffed the cold metal in his back waistband and walked toward the dance studio.

The familiar sonar ping on his phone alerted him of an incoming text. With his head on a swivel he returned to the car. A smile spread across his lips as he read Ariel's' message.

—*Hi T. One kitten left so I put dibs on the little dude. Forwarding his picture to you. Cute and needy. Ring a bell?*—

He laughed out loud before texting his reply.

—*Who me? No way. Thanks, Ariel*—

As the incoming image came into focus, his mind somersaulted and his eyes did a double take. A steel gray beauty with green eyes stared back.

Tony didn't believe in fate. He believed in creating his own future, but this coincidence couldn't be denied. The kitten, a perfect duplicate of the pet he'd adored as a child, sealed the idea in his mind of a cosmic connection between him and Sierra.

As if the cosmos was on board with the timing, Sierra opened the glass door to the studio and zeroed in on him with a querying expression and mouthed, "What happened?"

He smiled and started toward her but was cut off by a string of familiar cars streaming into the asphalt lot, maneuvering into parking slots like synchronized swimmers. Tony raised his shoulders in a gesture of surrender and backed up to lean against the hood. The children were loaded into the cars and soon the parking lot was empty again. Sierra closed and locked the studio door before crossing the parking lot. She opened the driver's door, hopped in without a word and held her hand out the window for the keys.

Uh oh, I might have stepped into a small pile of poopy by not going inside like I promised.

He wasted no time getting in the passenger seat, when she pushed the ignition button and roared the engine to life, eyes fixed straight ahead. Without being prompted and with the hope of short cutting any recriminations, he said, "An important phone call."

She turned off the engine and faced him. "Dare I ask the nature of said call?"

"You could, but if I told you, I'd have to kill you."

She balled her fist and punched his thigh. "In your wildest dreams."

Secretly pleased her feistiness returned, he leaned over, raised her hand to his lips and placed a tender kiss on her palm. "Baby, my wildest dreams might include tying you up, but I'd never hurt you."

She held her sides while her shoulders shook. "What is this, fifty shades of Navy?"

"Okay, smart ass." He jabbed his index finger in

her ribs. "I have a little surprise for you if you can stop laughing at your own joke long enough to listen to me."

Sierra jerked to attention, her right hand in a playful salute and her left hand splayed across her mouth in an obvious attempt to thwart the snickers.

Tony dismantled her salute and removed her hand before capturing her full lips with his teeth. He then invaded her mouth with his tongue. She returned the heat without hesitation and he started to understand what sex in a parking lot might be like. Withdrawing his tongue but maintaining feather-light contact with her lips, he whispered, "We're going on a road trip."

She pulled back and gasped, her eyes wide. "I love road trips."

"How does Orlando sound? I've located a spectacularly romantic hotel…with room service."

"When?"

"Now. Start the engine."

"I don't have any clothes packed." She pressed the ignition button, snugged the seat belt around her and connected the ends with a snap. Then, sniffed under her arm. "And I need a shower. I'm gross."

"You won't need any clothes," he said. "One other thing. I read there's a tub big enough for two in the room." The way her face flushed with his suggestion ignited his imagination with all the things they would do. His already light-hearted mood blossomed at the prospect of having Sierra Sanchez naked and in his arms all weekend.

Chapter Fifteen

While they drove toward Orlando and Sierra related techniques for teaching the Salsa to children, Tony checked the side view mirror with casual but regular glances. *Was that the same car keeping pace behind them?*

All that could be determined from this distance was the driver was male with a beard and the passenger, smaller stature with long hair, was almost certainly a female. He dismissed any threat. *Calculated guess, a farmer and his wife.*

"So, the kids get confused on which is left and which is right, so I named the right foot, cookies and the left foot, milk." She released her grip on the steering wheel to demonstrate the basic technique and rolled hers arms in concise circles, "Cookies and milk, cookies and milk."

Tony steadied the wheel with his left hand while Sierra continued to configure her arms in precise Zumba moves as they barreled down the highway. His lips stretched into a broad smile. Her enthusiasm for life blew him away.

****

As they eased the car around the circular, portico-covered brick entrance of the Grand Bohemian Hotel, Sierra gazed in awe at the contemporary fifteen storied building. "How did you find such a perfect place?"

"I have my ways." He pressed the unlock button while the valet scampered around the front bumper and opened her door. Tony climbed out and flung the duffel bag over his shoulder. Although she didn't observe the action, Sierra was certain he'd discreetly secured his concealed weapon somewhere on his body.

The valet shuffled to the rear compartment. "No luggage," Tony said as Sierra dangled the keys in the air for the valet.

As the uniformed man hurried to retrieve them, she worried that the gesture conveyed snobbery and a pang of embarrassment swept over her. She handed him the keys with a warm smile, then reached into her jacket pocket for a tip, but Tony was already slipping a twenty-dollar bill into the surprised man's palm. Then, with his hand in the small of her back he pressed her forward, past the magnificent ebony horse sculpture gracing the front entrance. A livery-clad doorman wearing a pleasant expression held open the etched-glass door and welcomed them through the threshold.

Sierra uttered "nice" under her breath as her eyes wandered around the lobby and perused the stunning art collection hanging from every wall while Tony checked in. Her gaze traveled up to the barrel-vaulted ceilings covered in Italian mosaic tile. "OMG."

Within minutes of arriving, his arms wrapped around her waist and the pale gold room key card magically rose to eye level. For someone trained in the art of killing, she mused, his soft side showed itself with little effort and if she was honest with herself, irresistibly. She leaned into his embrace. "What an oasis."

His breath blew on her ear and sent sensual chills

down the length of her body. "Hungry?"

"What did you have in mind?" She shivered and rubbed her bare arms as he passed the elevator key over the security pad.

"Room service and a fluffy warm robe for you." The door opened and he waited while she entered first. As the door slid shut, Tony hauled her backwards into his chest and briskly massaged her arms. "The big enough for two, jacuzzi tub I told you about is in the next room, if you're interested."

"So many choices." She clucked several times, then added. "I could use a bath after this morning's class and a glass of wine would be heaven."

"Done and done," he said.

The elevator bumped to a stop on the tenth floor. Tony stepped out and glanced in both directions before allowing Sierra to exit. "We're right here." He pointed to the room directly to the right of the elevator entrance. He grabbed her hand and tugged her the few steps to the room. With his other hand he inserted the key in the slot until the light flicked green and then pushed open the door, indicating with a wave of his hand for her to enter first.

Sierra's stomach lurched with the click of room number 1010 unlocking. The magnitude of risk-taking shouldered by this beautiful man, all so they could be alone together, settled in and she shivered.

Her thoughts, possessed by long-quiet demons, urged her to run like hell. She braced her arms on either side of the doorway. Dating Tony now, in these circumstances, with a possible threat close by, conjured up all too familiar memories of fear and an uncertain future. To deny those feelings, however, meant the return of an emptiness she'd endured too long.

"What the hell are we doing here?" she asked over her shoulder.

"You don't like it?" Tony, clearly confused by her sudden change in attitude, peered into the room.

"You're being hunted by crazy-assed assassins who could be anywhere, even here in Florida, even made it to Orlando." Her voice squeaked as it rose. "And I'm your booty-call for the weekend?"

Tony glanced up and down the hall before placing his index finger on Sierra's lips. "This is more to me than, as you call it, a booty call. I want to spend time with you." He had the door braced open with one arm. "But if you're worried about my safety, we should probably move our conversation into the room." He nodded toward the interior.

As Sierra slid forward into the room, past Tony's muscled bicep stretched above her, he released the door and swatted her behind. His palpable air of self-confidence intimidated and intrigued her. She couldn't decide whether his behavior was rational or reckless or a combination of the two, but the heat radiating between her legs spiraled to her knotted stomach and was…so real.

A breathtaking view of the city drew her to the wall length windows. "Nice choice. It's so quiet to be right in the heart of the performing arts district."

"Glad you approve. I've never been here before either, but I have it on good authority, you'd like this place. I'll bet a glass of wine would enhance the experience." He checked the label on a bottle of wine cooling in a bucket of ice before pulling a knife from his pocket.

"Are you going to open the bottle with that?"

A corkscrew appeared, and he threaded the pointed bottom into the plugged top. "Of course." She thrust her palms out and snorted. "A knife with a corkscrew attached. What else?"

"This little baby is a Swiss Army knife and every self-respecting warrior carries one." Tony wiggled out the cork and poured two goblets of wine. As he placed one in her outstretched hand, he raised his eyebrow. "It wouldn't hurt you to learn a few survival skills"

"Sure." She gulped. "Whatever."

The real reason she fled Colombia as a teenager and requested political asylum in the U.S. involved a catalog of survival skills. Leaving had been her only choice after providing what she thought was a confidential statement against the guerrilla leader of a revolutionary force. As it turned out, corruption in her country was more widespread than her family realized. The statement disappeared, the charges were dropped, and the death threats started. Tony didn't need to be clued into how well she understood death threats. She'd closed that chapter of her life a long time ago.

"You okay? You drifted off for a minute."

"A little tired but a nice hot bath…ummm."

He waggled his eyebrows. "Want some company?"

Sierra stood and beckoned him with a finger and a half-smile. "Like minds."

"Joined hearts," he murmured, following her into the bathroom.

****

Within seconds of a sharp rap on the door, Tony untangled himself from the arms of a sleeping Sierra and reached for the gun under his pillow. Last night was the hottest sex of his life, confirming what he'd suspected since first laying eyes on her. She was his one and only for all time.

The second distinct knock signaled the presence of a trusted friend on the other side and, considering the time of night, bearing an important message. He grabbed his T-shirt from the foot of the bed, tossed it over his head and yanked on his jeans before cracking open the door.

In a low whisper he greeted Pudge. "Yo, bro, step inside but quiet," he nodded toward the silhouette curled up in the bed.

"I hope you had enough fun to last you awhile." His voice subdued but audible. "Cause we gotta go."

Tony peered over his shoulder at Sierra. "Give me a minute." He withdrew a piece of hotel stationary and a pen from the desk drawer.

Sleeping beauty,

I arranged for breakfast in bed at eight a.m. Thought we'd be sleeping in. I've taken care of the bill. Enjoy. Sorry I can't be here to share it with you.

Don't worry. I'll be back soon, and we'll enjoy many more (fill in the blank) nights together like last night. There's a present waiting for you at your house.

Tony

P.S. I filled in the blank with, "unforgettable."

He propped the note on the empty pillow, slung the duffel over one shoulder and blew her a kiss before slipping through the door. Pudge stretched around Tony and nudged the door closed until the lock clicked.

"This is déjà vu all over again," Tony said with a sigh, remembering a previous midnight departure from the hospital.

Pudge patted Tony's shoulder. "Sorry man."

"Sorry doesn't begin to describe not waking up next to her," he said between gritted teeth. "I'm going to kill those bastards."

Pudge nodded and led the way into the elevator. They rode down in silence, and emerged, radiating an alpha aura of all business.

Light-footed and swift they faded into the night…for the second time.

Chapter Sixteen

"Damn it." Sierra tossed the pillow across the room then reread Tony's note.

"There's never going to be anything normal about this relationship." She crumpled the piece of paper and launched it toward the trashcan. "I don't need presents." Fuming, she paced across the suite. "What I need is a stable relationship with someone who isn't bouncing in and out of my life."

An abrupt knock on the door startled her out of an incipient rant. A male voice called out, "Room service."

She checked the time. Eight a.m. Tony's note said the food would arrive at eight.

She started toward the door and froze. *What if it's not room service? What if the killers followed us?* She picked up the hotel phone and dialed zero, then hesitated. *Geez, I'm becoming paranoid.* In a nervous rush, she slid the handset back in the cradle and tiptoed to the door.

A second knock, followed by an enunciated, "Room Service," reverberated through the door.

The chain lock hung unattached. Sierra clutched her chest to quiet the pounding against her ribs. After inhaling a deep breath, she attached the chain in one fluid movement and cracked open the door. A young, clean-cut male with the required five-star smile presented the room service tray. She peered at his name tag and uniform. Both displayed the logo of the hotel and appeared legit. She removed the chain and flung open the door, silently chiding herself.

The server carried in the breakfast tray and held it out from his body as an offering. "Where would you like it set up?"

She pointed to a round table by the window. "Over there is fine." The smell of bacon enticed her as the waiter passed by.

After placing the tray where she indicated and removing the plate covers with a flourish, he asked, "Do you need anything else, ma'am?"

"No." She replied with a fake smile. "Do I need to sign anything?"

"No, ma'am. All taken care of." He bowed and wished her a pleasant day before exiting the room.

She locked the door behind him and shuddered. The situation with Tony affected her more than she realized. Her emotions ricocheted between giddy excitement when he was nearby to nervous anxiety over what could occur next. Famished, she stuffed a piece of bacon in her mouth and grabbed a sip of coffee but left the remaining eggs, toast and hash browns for two, untouched, determined her best source of security lay in the solace of her own space.

Rounding up her sparse belongings she snatched the last piece of bacon and dropped it in her mouth before surveying the space one final time for anything left behind. With a wistful gaze, she stared at the jacuzzi where a bubble bath had escalated into a game of Duck, Duck, Goose, well at least the goose part. They both laughed so hard when Tony entered the tub clutching a rubber duck and even harder when the duck floated atop the waves they created. Sense of humor was on her top five list of must have attributes for a mate and Tony had a lightning fast wit. Now, the rubber toy perched on the corner of the tub, a lifeless stare on its plastic face.

She spun on her heels, shutting the bathroom door behind her, choking back a sob. She hated herself for being so conflicted. Before she changed her mind again, she raced back into the bathroom, grabbed the damn duck and stuffed him in her Zumba bag. Then, she headed straight for the valet station where she handed over her parking ticket to attentive staff along with the expected tip.

While waiting for them to retrieve her car, she tapped the toe of her shoe and glanced around for anything or anyone unusual. Nothing seemed out of the ordinary. Tapping her toes always calmed her and *yes*, as the car pulled up to the curb, made the car appear sooner. She hopped in, tuned to her favorite dance channel and pulled the duck from her bag.

"You can help me drive," she said with a snort before speeding toward the interstate and home.

****

Relieved and somehow reassured at the crunch of her tires against the gravel in her driveway, Sierra shifted her attention from the mental hamster wheel spinning inside her head, to discovering the surprise Tony left. The enigma surrounding him churned up her thoughts and apple-carted her emotions.

She dropped her overstuffed bag on the tiled foyer floor and peered in the living room, anticipating flowers or maybe a plant. *Nope.* The quiet in the house was almost eerie except for the metronomic tick, tick, tick

116

of a desk clock. There was light streaming from the kitchen, and she didn't remember leaving lights on, so she leaned against one side of the wall as she tiptoed down the short hall…*What the heck?*

A muted cry greeted her as she entered the room. In the corner, between the refrigerator and the bar was a large brown mover's box. A small meow squeaked from inside the box.

"Oh My God!" She caught her breath. "He didn't." She peered over the side and exhaled, "Oh, yes he did."

"Hello," she cooed.

Wide, curious green eyes stared back. "Meow."

"Come here, you little cutie." The kitten purred as she lifted the silky gray bundle into her arms.

Bold, block lettering she didn't recognize, printed on the side of the box caught her eye as she stepped back. *In case you get lonely.*

Sierra hugged the kitten against her chest and heaved a deep sigh as the hamster wheel in her head renewed its mental spin.

Chapter Seventeen

"The trucks are parked right where Sierra's uncle said they'd be," Pudge said. "Good sign."

"I wasn't worried. Per Sierra, her uncle served in the United States military. After talking on the phone a few times and having a video chat with him, I sensed he was reliable," he paused, "and crafty. Witness his idea of a meeting place." Tony pointed with his thumb at twelve parked eighteen-wheelers, with rainbow-colored Sanchez Brothers Circus decals plastered on each. "An I-75 rest stop where the Sanchez Brothers circus convoy usually parks is nothing unusual."

"Shrewd. I agree. What does he look like?"

"Like him." Tony pointed toward a muscular, middle-aged man with light brown skin who climbed down from the closest tractor-trailer and bee-lined for their pickup.

Pudge exited first and checked both directions before nodding to Tony who grabbed his gear bag from the rear and hopped to the ground. Pudge's hand hung loose by his side, within easy reach of the 9mm Sig Sauer tucked and hidden under his loose shirt.

"Be cool, Pudge," Tony warned.

"Always am, brother."

Tony stuck out his hand. "Alejandro, I take it?"

"Alex is fine." The man smiled broadly and gripped Tony's offered hand in a firm shake. "You're

Sierra's friend?"

Pudge cleared his throat with a loud and noticeable harrumph.

"I am," Tony said with a side glance at Pudge. "Friends. Alex, meet Bill Evanston."

The men shook hands and checked each other out like two bantam roosters. Tony decided it was time to go. "Don't want to hold you up, man. Ready to roll out? Pudge, keep me apprised."

"Will do." Pudge leaned in and whacked Tony's back before stepping into his pickup truck and cranking up the engine. As he drove away, Pudge smacked the door panel in a double slap goodbye and sped off.

Tony inhaled a deep breath, picked up his bag and walked in silence beside the man he now entrusted with his life.

****

During the three-hour trip to Jacksonville, Florida, the first stop on the tour, Tony developed his cover story with Alex while the driver chatted on his CB radio. They decided he'd use his middle name, Joseph, for a last name in case someone Googled the new trainer out of curiosity. Social media forums didn't exist when Tony first became a SEAL, or he would have been ordered to wipe them clean. Regardless, he decided not to be a part of the social media scene after he got out of the military. Lucky for him, he liked privacy, because any new postings were prime tracking tools used by both sides.

He didn't want to draw attention to his sudden appearance in the circus but the convenient fact that the previous horse trainer quit, facilitated by Alex paying the guy a bundle to vamoose, left an opening. Tony's chest tightened, humbled by the guy's willingness to help him. Sierra had shared Alex's story of immigrating here in his early twenties with hope of a better life. He was tough and good at what he did. He'd achieved his dream of owning his own business and gave credit to living in America for his success. No arguing this guy was a true patriot.

"First, we handle the horses and then we get you settled in, Tony. Follow me," Alex said with a slight but detectable accent. A few feet ahead, he veered off toward a large horse trailer. The horses stamped and whinnied their impatience as the two men approached. "Ever worked with Andalusians?"

"Mostly quarter horses in Texas but I'm game."

"So are they." Alex smiled. "From Spanish descent, hot-blooded but easy to work with, intelligent and athletic. We have a total of twelve. We'll unload this truck first, then feed, water and house the horses in the stalls here at the fairground for tonight."

Alex shifted to the side door of the trailer and slid open the large metal latch. The smell of sweet alfalfa hay intermingled with fresh horse manure wafted down the ramp as Alex gestured for Tony to join him inside the trailer.

Six of the finest specimens of horseflesh Tony had ever seen waited in small, individual cubicles. Pearl colored coats with flowing manes and tails adorned sturdy, rounded bodies. He patted the first muscular neck as he entered, "Easy, boy."

He continued the hand contact until he reached the halter. The horse nuzzled Tony's head and nickered a welcome. *I've still got it.* He rubbed the horse's face while Alex untied the halter, then snapped on the lead rope and handed him off to Tony who guided him, without a hitch, down the ramp.

Tony handed the lead to a blonde nymph with braided hair hanging halfway down her back and crystal blue eyes that he swore, twinkled. *Where did she come from…out of the blue…in stealth mode?*

She stuck out a hand. "Hi. I'm Candi."

Yes, you are. "Nice to meet you. I'm Tony, the new horse trainer."

He clasped her hand and inhaled her scent, which like her name exuded the heady, hot sweetness of cotton candy. The strength of her return grip surprised him as did her reluctant release when he tried to reclaim his hand.

"I'm one of the trick riders so I guess we'll be working together." She dropped his hand and tied the corners of the blue chambray shirttail under her breasts exposing a diamond piercing in her belly button. *Good Lord. He hoped working together didn't imply what her body language suggested.*

He took a fast glance around the unenclosed area near the main tent."Are you part of a troupe?"

"Yes." She positioned her thumbs in the waistband of her painted-on Daisy Duke shorts, forcing anyone who had eyes to focus on the lacy fringe of her underwear playing peek a boo. "My two older brothers, my father and my twin sister all ride."

There are two of you? Pointing to the barn, he asked, "How about storing this guy in one of the stalls while I unload the next one?" He tossed her the lead rope and withdrew up the ramp where Alex waited with another horse. Several clucks urged the horse forward, followed by the clip clop of hoofs.

"Tony, I need to supervise the tent raisings," Alex said. "You have this under control, right?"

Dude, you could have warned me. "Yeah. Definitely. Under control. All good."

The staccato response had Alex leaning around the corner of the truck with a quizzical expression. He smiled and gave Tony a thumb's up.

Alex made a backhand wave and bellowed orders at the tent crew as he scurried off. The circus buzzed with the activity of an ant colony as metal poles levitated into position while a dozen men hammered stakes in the ground. A crew of synchronized workers, using guy wires, hoisted the candy apple red and white-striped canvas tops.

The nymph waited, curling a lock of hair around her index finger, while he brought out the next horse. Without speaking, he handed her the lead and ducked into the trailer for another Spanish beauty. The silent hand-off continued until the final horse, a young stallion and the only black member of the team was unloaded.

The scents of hickory bar-b-que sauce and garlic butter wafted over the air, beckoning him. *Ahhh. The cooks finally started dinner. Time to find some chow.*

Tony followed the smoke curling up from behind one of the plain canvas tents and entered through the tied back tent flaps of the circus mess hall. His stomach growled and cramped. He remembered the last time he ate; last night with Sierra. He already missed her and was slightly curious as to why he'd heard nothing from her. Not even a text thanking him for her *purry* little present. He decided to give her a call on the burner phone after dinner.

With a full plate of sliced brisket atop a piece of garlic bread he slid onto the first free bench at an empty picnic table inside the mess hall. As he picked up his fork, his phone vibrated in his pants pocket. He retrieved the phone and viewed one missed text from a private number. The only people who had this number were cleared to have this number. He hit redial.

"Can I join you?" Candi smiled, presenting her tray as evidence she needed a place to sit.

Tony ended the call. "Sure," and surreptitiously stuffed the phone back in his pocket.

She sat, almost on top of him, her bare leg connecting with his khaki trousers. "Thanks."

His left leg bounced up and down as he scooped a fork full of beef. He popped the food into his mouth and scooted an inch to the right.

Candi turned toward him. Her cherry-colored lips quirked up at the ends as she asked, "What brought you here to the circus?"

An ISIS hit squad. "Horses," he said after a quick swallow.

She blew a breath up, parting her blonde bangs that hung in a sexy drape over her eyebrows. "You don't need to tell me your whole life story but horses? That's it. Just horses?"

"Pretty much." *And someone trying to collect the bounty on my head.*

"How do you know Alex?" She took a gulp from the bottle of sparkling water, then crinkled up her nose. "Fizz shot up my nose."

"A mutual friend."

"Uh-huh." She flipped her braid behind her shoulder. "You have some sauce." She pointed to a speck on the chest area of his shirt.

Tony glanced down. "Oh." He grabbed a napkin off the table, but she swiped at his hand.

"Allow me." She angled her chin toward a tumbler she held. "I have the seltzer water." Dipping the edge of her napkin into the glass, she closed the distance Tony had deftly put between them. With one hand on his thigh she leveraged her nimble body into the curve of his shoulder, her breast grazing his chest as she made small circular motions on the tiny spot. "All gone."

"Thanks."

Candi unfolded her athletic legs and stood, arching her back, thrusting her breasts forward. "Need any help setting up your quarters?"

He had a feeling their definitions of "help setting up your quarters" were vastly different. His throat tightened. Her tone and body language screamed, "Want to get naked with me?" but before he could answer, his pants vibrated again.

He stood and retrieved the phone and his earpiece. *Sierra.* "I need to take this call." With a brief nod, he mouthed, "Later," and quick-stepped out of the mess hall while plugging in his earpiece.

"Hey, baby. You okay?"

The sound of her "yes" had him breathing hard. "I'm smitten with my kitten. Thank you."

"You're welcome. I hear purring. Where is he?"

"Nestled under my chin. He's so adorable and sweet."

"Have you named him yet?"

"No, but he gives off the vibe of a McTavish."

Tony smiled. *What the heck is a McTavish vibe?* "Excellent choice."

124

Aware there was an elephant in the room, in addition to a fur ball named McTavish and the fact she wasn't going to bring it up, he decided to dive in. "Sorry I had to leave the party so abruptly. Are you mad at me?"

"I figured you must have a good reason to…you know…. Tony, this is all new to me. I've never dated a guy with your past…or present. It's interesting." Her voice quavered. "Annoying, confusing and scary."

Gut check. Was she crying? "You realize this is temporary, right? As soon as the guys get a fix on the whereabouts of the bad actors…"

"Stop." She sniffled. "That's the whole point. You're living under this dark, ugly cloud and I'm sharing the ugly with you. The danger feels real."

"No shit, Sherlock." His words snapped through his lips in quick bursts. Fear of another abandonment drove his anger.

"The problem is I care about you, Tony, but I have a very public life, a life I love as a nationally known Zumba instructor."

The burn of acid dread crawled up his throat. "What are you saying?"

"Maybe we should take a break until this is over." Her voice broke on the last couple of words.

Bile touched his tongue. He swallowed hard. "Are you breaking up with me?"

"No, no…well, maybe but just until this whole thing is over. It's temporary. I want to feel safe and I don't. I'm afraid for you and what could happen to you and to me."

"You better make up your mind, Sierra. You're either in or you're out but before you answer, understand if you say, we're done, we're done forever and not on vacation."

"I don't like being pressured."

"I don't like being abandoned, I—I mean jacked around, Sierra."

She inhaled a deep, choppy breath. "This whole thing is making me a basket case."

"What thing?"

"Are you being intentionally dense? The death threat, of course. I'm feeling uncertain and even afraid about the future."

He snorted. "No. Listen sweetie. I'm in this with you for the long haul, good or bad. I can't, no—" he corrected himself. "I don't *want* to do it without you."

She sighed. "You got me. I guess the stress is getting to me."

"So, we good?"

"We're good but why is it taking so long to locate these guys? I don't get it."

"The best analogy I can give you is the FBI's Most Wanted List. Some of those losers remain on their list for years."

"But you guys haven't even informed the FBI about the situation."

"Gavin put feelers out to a friend in Ocala. They have an inkling these guys are in Florida but no actual intel on exactly where they are. Until we locate them or they do something threatening, we're good."

"I wish I was there with you," Sierra said, her voice solemn and quiet.

"I wish you were with me too but not if it puts your safety at risk." His next thought was interrupted when he sensed someone approaching. He stiffened, then relaxed when he recognized the intruder.

Candi, twisting a lock of hair around her index finger in an aged coy come-on said, "Tony, sorry to interrupt but are we having practice today or what?"

"Yes. I'll be right in." He nodded toward the tent. "Do me a favor and get the other riders."

"My sister's on vacation," she replied. "But I'll make sure my brothers are there."

He mouthed thank you to Candi, then made shooing motions with one hand. Into the phone he said, "Gotta run, babe, but I'll call again soon." Silence. "You okay?"

"Yes, go do what you need to do," Sierra replied, a hint of resignation in her voice.

"Bye for now," he said and pulled the earpiece from his ear.

"Tony?" Sierra said with apparent urgency.

"Yeah?" He rammed the rubber back in his ear canal, wincing from the amount of force he'd used.

"Did I hear a woman's voice, a young woman's voice, talking to you?"

"Yeah."

"Who is she?"

"Someone with shitty timing."

Chapter Eighteen

Four weeks later

Sierra clamped her hand over her mouth as she raced for the toilet. Her breakfast protein shake, bland as cardboard, rode back up her throat like a souped-up go-cart. Tail erect and flicking back and forth like a metronome, McTavish followed, zigzagging between furniture legs. He leaped on the bathroom counter and peered over the edge as she slammed the commode top upright and bent at the waist.

After vomiting her breakfast, she dry-heaved until tears rolled down her cheeks. She rested her pounding head on the shower door and with her eyes closed, groped for the hand towel on the bar to her right. Using the soft bamboo cloth, she blotted the damp heat from her face and neck. *What she would give for a cold drink of bottled water?*

She opened her eyes and raised her head, peering at her reflection in the mirror. "Ugh! I'm a mess, McTavish." He answered with a comforting purr and nudge to her arm.

"I suspect last night's fish might have been last week's catch." As she attempted to stand, her knees buckled. She grabbed the corner of the vanity and hauled herself upright. Shaky and weak, she used the wall for support and headed for the bedroom to lie down for a few minutes. McTavish trotted along, keeping pace with her movement and, she sensed, her dilemma.

****

"Hey, Kate, can you help me with tonight's Zumba class?"

Sierra held the phone away from her as she swallowed the bile filling her throat and swiped her hand across the beads of sweat dampening her forehead. Her classes were high intensity, but Kate, an accountant by day, was a certified, bad-ass instructor in the physically demanding work-out. She was also a perennial friend and roommate at annual conventions.

"I was planning a late night at the office, doing some number crunching but sure, what's up?"

Sierra leaned against the doorjamb into the bathroom, using it for balance as well as support. "Lost my breakfast shake this morning and I've been woozy all day."

"Oh no. Do you think it's the flu?"

"Maybe, but I don't have a fever and nothing…you know…no other problems. I was thinking food poisoning. Any food odors make me want to throw up."

"Stay home, rest," Kate said. "I'll rock your class."

"You sure?"

"Yes, you've subbed for me before and it's not like the girls are cliquey. They're always welcoming and fun. Besides, I'd much rather exercise my body than tax my mind."

Sierra squeaked out a muffled laugh despite how much she wanted to barf. "Very funny Kate and nice play on words for a corporate accountant."

"Feel better, Sierra."

"I'm headed for bed as soon as we hang up. You're the best. Thanks!"

McTavish brushed against Sierra's leg and purred as she hit the end call button. "Okay buddy, let's feed you so I can drag my behind to bed."

The blast of air escaping the refrigerator cooled her face and neck as she leaned in for the cat food. She hung in the opening for a few seconds before retrieving the can of food and shutting the door. As she scooped a few tablespoons into the bowl, the pungent aroma of salmon wafted to her nostrils. Her stomach rolled in protest. "Good thing you inhale your soft food, Tavi." Sierra said, pinching her nostrils shut. As if in agreement, McTavish's purr grew more intense.

Satisfied her kitten would survive without her for a few hours of much needed sleep, Sierra placed her hands along the wall to help steady her as she made her way to her bedroom and the comfort of cotton sheets.

The next morning, she awoke to the same fire burning in her roiling gut. The queasy sensation demanded she dash for the bathroom. "What is this, frigging Ground Hog Day?" She flopped back into bed.

Her phone vibrated and Ariel's name appeared on the screen. Not sure if she was contagious and certain her friend would insist on coming over, she let the call go to voice mail. The desire for sleep overwhelmed her. She curled into a fetal position and drifted into dreamland.

****

When the deadbolt on the front door clicked open, Sierra sat up ramrod straight in the bed. She clutched the sheets to her chest and held her breath, listening for a second sound. A few seconds ticked by. The door closed with a familiar creak, followed by a shuffle of feet across the tile floor. "Hello?" Her voice wobbled.

"Sierra? Are you here?"

She breathed a sigh of relief when she recognized Ariel's voice, her best friend in the universe, who had arrived at just the right moment.

"In the bedroom but I think I have the flu, don't come back here."

"Too late," Ariel said as she paused in the doorway of the bedroom and groaned. "Uhhh, you're a pitiful sight. Like death warmed over. I'll get a cold washcloth." She ducked into the adjoining bathroom and called out, "What's going on?"

"I can't keep anything down."

Ariel returned, a wet cloth in her hand and perched on the side of the bed. "For how long?" she asked as she smoothed the cool fabric across Sierra's brow.

"Two days and counting."

"Any fever?"

"No. Ugh! Gotta go." She tossed back the covers and raced for the toilet.

Ariel stood in the bathroom doorway. "Girlfriend. You need to go to the doctor."

Sierra dragged herself back to the bed and flopped on top of the covers, wiggling in slow motion under the soft cotton. "I could use some water."

"Sure, and I'll make you burned toast. Back in a jiff." She patted Sierra's leg and eased off the bed. "Be a good girl and rest," she teased, rolling her eyes and simultaneously tilting her head.

Sierra heard the ping of the toaster followed shortly by the whoosh of the refrigerator door. Burnt toast and cold water appealed to her about as much as the slime on okra and boiled liver but if it could abate her nausea then she'd willingly consume an entire loaf.

Ariel, in what Sierra assumed was an attempt to make her laugh, paraded into the room like a server in a five-star restaurant, holding the plate level with her head, the bottle of water precariously balanced next to a single piece of burnt toast. Impromptu and funny, she let out a restrained laugh while Ariel placed the plate on the bedside table and secured the bottle of water in Sierra's outstretched hand.

After a quick gulp of water, she bit off the corner of the toast, chewed a little and swallowed. Aside from a low rumble, her stomach offered no protest. She continued nibbling small portions, intermixed with swigs of the water until both were gone. "Good news. Burnt toast isn't making me heave," she said, then burped.

"Feel better?"

"Yes, doctor. You don't have to stay. I can take care of myself from here. I think the worst is over."

"Promise, if you're not completely better by tomorrow, you'll go see your doctor or at least go to a walk-in clinic."

"I promise," she said, her hand over her heart.

"You usually get the cold sweats at the mention of seeing a doctor, so I expect a phone call afterward." Ariel gathered her purse and headed for the door. She stopped short of the threshold and said, "By the way, Gavin and I are working on having a bambino and I wanted you to be the first to hear the news."

Sierra sat up in bed and beamed, "So, so happy for you. Dibs on the baby shower."

Ariel nodded in agreement and put her hand to her

ear, "Call me."

When the front door closed with a clunk, Sierra laid her head on the cool pillow. She rubbed her stomach in a happy gesture for her friend's news and projected what a pregnant Ariel's life would encompass. Then her mind exploded with an epiphany; she couldn't remember when she'd had her last period.

Jesus. Where's my calendar?

She ripped off the covers and despite being weak-kneed, bouncing from wall to wall, she scurried into her office, hell-bent on locating her appointment book where she recorded her entire life, including the start date for each month's menstrual cycle. Flipping through the pages of the last month, she found the expected arrival date for her period.

Nooooo. The date of her last cycle was two months ago, two whole months. She collapsed in the swivel mesh chair.

McTavish leaped onto her lap and with an air of authority, walked his paws up Sierra's torso, stretched and dropped in her lap again, gently head-butting her elbow. She rubbed his ears and scratched under his chin until a loud hum erupted from his chest. "You need food little buddy?" The cat meowed. She lifted him on her shoulder, his favorite ride along spot and using the wide armrest as a lever, forced herself up.

After a forward sway, she steadied herself and headed for the kitchen. "Food first, then you watch the house while I drive to the nearest drugstore."

****

"Miss, your change."

"Huh? Oh, thank you." Sierra halted her exit and grabbed the money from the clerk's out-stretched hand.

In a rush to get home and self-administer the pregnancy test, she stuffed the bills in the pocket of her jacket and put the coins in her wallet, forgetting to zip shut the coin compartment. As she began to fold the wallet, the coins spilled on the counter, the floor, and rolled down the aisle. A woman behind her who appeared out of nowhere, stooped to help and collected most of the quarters while Sierra retrieved the dimes and nickels.

"Here you go, miss," the stranger said as she handed Sierra the change. Her lips thinned into a forced smile.

Sierra detected an accent but couldn't place the exact origin and except for the dark-colored scarf covering her head, the woman dressed in typical American jeans and long-sleeved, collared shirt.

"Thanks for your help," Sierra said, but a shiver ran up her spine. Something about the woman's eyes gave her pause. They held no joy, no spark and as the saying alleged about the eyes being the windows to the soul…well…nobody home.

But the woman stopped to help her when no one else in the store bothered so she discounted the sudden chill as a physical leftover from her recent illness. At least, she hoped like hell the reaction was virus born and not first born.

****

Her pants fell around her ankles as she entered the hallway leading to the bathroom.

Already divested of keys, purse and jacket she held the pregnancy test in her teeth and thumbed her underwear on both sides, removing them in one swift movement as she reached the commode. Sierra slid the plastic tester under her and squatted. When finished, she gripped the handle, holding the cylinder inches from her face, but her hand was shaking so she steadied it on the counter and hovered.

Minute after painful minute passed while her mind raced with thoughts of how a simple plus symbol might alter her life in such a drastic way. Tony. How would he react? Maybe the outcome would be negative, and she would never, ever again have unprotected sex, no matter how mind-blowing.

Time up. She opened one eye and peeked.

A pink plus sign showed.

She jiggled the tester. *Still plus.* The off-white walls appeared closer and there wasn't enough air to breathe. She opened the single window in the room and plastered her head against the screen, breathing in deep gulps of the humid Florida air. The warmth somehow comforted her, and she sucked through her mouth, inhaling, exhaling, inhaling, exhaling.

Maybe I overreacted? Maybe I misread the result?

Resolved to tackle the life changes a positive stick symbol would set into motion, she inhaled a final breath and swung her head back in the room. *Yep. The result hasn't changed.* She closed her eyes and pinched the bridge of her nose. When she opened them, she stared at herself in the counter-to-ceiling-mirror and tried to picture a bulging belly with a protruding navel in work-out clothes. *Nope. She couldn't.*

And where was Tony in her mocked-up future?

She'd have to tell him as he most definitely spawned this baby but first, she'd need to confirm the drugstore test with a blood test in a doctor's office. With so many thoughts darting around in her head, she needed a to-do list, a baby-do list. She smiled at the term she coined as she rubbed her stomach in circular motions, an ancient instinct. Maybe a bite to eat would quiet the flip, roll, flip, while she worked on her list. The relentless nausea, which had plagued her for the past few days, subsided. Convinced discovery of the true cause made it tolerable, she experienced relief.

Food. I need food...for two.

Chapter Nineteen

Surprised at the level of luxury his assigned digs offered, Tony dropped his bag on the hardwood floor and rotated like a periscope. His sumptuous quarters, located in the front compartment of the horse trailer, but strangely void of any lingering horse smell, sported a kitchen equipped with wood cabinets, an oven with stove top, refrigerator and what? Whaddya know, a microwave.

On the opposite side of the room, a U-shaped booth with cushioned oak benches served as an eating area. He eased down the length of the trailer into a living space with a jack-knife bed and a small flat screen television. Walking past a bathroom complete with shower, he faced the last space, separated by a closed sliding door. With his palm flat on the surface, he cracked open a small space, then cupped the edge, and slid the door into the inset. A queen-sized Murphy bed filled most of the space leaving only a narrow footpath on three sides.

"The real meaning of bed…room." He dragged one hand across his face, feeling every day of his thirty-six years. "I must be more exhausted than I thought."

The bed was unmade but someone had left a set of organic cotton sheets along with two pillows. He did an about-face and fell backward on the hard mattress, raising his arms above his head. *Peace and Quiet*. His low back throbbed, and his shoulders ached. The thought of sleep beckoned. *First things first.* He rolled to the side of the bed, swung his feet to the floor and pushed himself up with a groan.

He positioned the bottom sheet on the four corners and fitted each section in place. Using hospital corners for the top sheet, he finished the bed by tugging the bedspread to the head of the mattress. Flopping backwards, he folded his arms under the back of his head and crossed his ankles. No one would miss him for a while.

He had made up some lame excuse for Candi and the other trick riders to add an extra practice session while he retreated to his digs solo. He needed time to think. His last conversation with Sierra was frankly weird. She'd transformed from revelry instigator at the wedding to an emotional roller coaster in their last phone call. Granted his situation created additional strain in their relationship. Guilt rode him like a two-hundred-pound gorilla for involving Sierra in his mess. Convincing her the anomaly of being hunted was only a squall, not a Category 5 hurricane, would require an in-person visit.

He needed to hold her, reassure her. *Stat.* Being separated only reinforced his desire to be with her. It wouldn't be hard to sneak out and drive the three hours to Gainesville. No one would miss him in the middle of the night. Well, that was debatable with Candi on the prowl. In earlier times in his life, he would have been flattered by the attention and challenged by the pursuit. Now, not so much. The whole idea of a superficial sex-fest bored him. *Why have a fling when I could spend honest time with someone easy to talk to and fun to be around?* He and Sierra had to get past the current situation and once this farce was behind him, he'd prove to her he was a regular guy.

He wasn't all-in on this hiding bullshit, but he'd had his arm-twisted by the guys. The disappearing act was supposed to be until they could locate the assassins and inform the FBI of their whereabouts, ensure they were in custody, and life goes on. From what Pudge had told him, they were making progress. He simply had to keep his head down a while longer.

In the meantime, an in-person conversation with Sierra would help sort out the difficulty of loving a man with a target on his back. He hoped.

Damn. His car was in Los Angeles in the repair shop. Too late to get a rental which also left a paper trail. Candi's car might be a possibility but was he willing to open Pandora's box by asking to borrow it overnight? He supposed he could tell her he needed a loaner for a couple of hours and would have it back before she woke up—and with a full tank of gas.

"Besides, she checks out my ass more than she'd ever check her mileage."

Tony popped up and rolled to his feet. Sleep could wait. He ducked into the bathroom and ran a hand through his hair as he checked his game face in the mirror. He tugged at the cotton hem of his khaki T-shirt and slipped on his work boots. After spotting Candi through the kitchen window, he shouldered the trailer door open and, in his rush, used more force than he intended. The frame slammed against the outside panel and the crash caught Candi's attention. Her head whipped around at the same time Tony exited.

"Hey, Candi." He waved his arm to call her over.

"I need a favor."

She ran her tongue around the rim of her mouth, emphasizing the fullness of her lips."Sure. What?"

He focused on his mission. "I'd like to borrow your car for a few hours."

"Don't you have one?"

"I do but it's in the repair shop." A coy smile spread across her lips as she clasped her hands behind her back thrusting out her chest. "I'll take you anywhere you want to go."

Yikes. Tony received the innuendo loud and clear but chose to play dumb. "Kind of you to offer but I'm leaving very early in the morning and I'd rather have you rested and fit to rehearse our act when I get back."

"Okay." The corners of her mouth drooped in obvious disappointment. "I'll get the keys." Rather than her usual bouncy step, she dragged her feet in a shuffle. Tony almost felt sorry for her.

Almost, that was—until he glimpsed into the future at her fantasy payback for this favor.

****

Tony parked down the street and on the opposite side from where his GPS had located Sierra's blue-trimmed bungalow. Headlights in her window at this hour might scare her and on the slim chance his whereabouts had been discovered and he'd been followed…well, suffice it to say, he wasn't taking any chances.

The street was quiet, no traffic, no lights from any of the homes, nothing to give him away as he hugged the shrub border in a crouched jog. At two a.m. the world was a strangely peaceful place.

Oak branches, with Spanish Moss dangling in

disarray, loomed over the empty driveway next to her house. A light breeze swept the tendrils in a back and forth shadow and lent the appearance of mythical gods or alien monsters, depending on your world view.

Odd, she didn't leave any lights on and where's her car? Tony ghosted to the back of the house and located with ease, the begonia-filled planter where she'd earlier told him she hid a spare key in a metal turtle. Brushing back the thick leaves, he found the tortoise, lodged deep in the dirt and retrieved the key. As he stepped back toward the door, he noticed the plantation blinds at the kitchen window were cracked opened. *That's odd.* Sierra had shown him multiple pictures of her house and its layout. From those photos and several conversations, he knew her awareness of security, as a woman living alone, was a plus ten. In a nightly ritual, blinds and curtains were closed at dark. He squatted and peeked between the blinds. The refrigerator had a night-light and he caught a movement. His hand whipped to the weapon in his waist band. A dash of gray leaped onto a bar stool and with a quick jump, hopped onto the counter near the sink.

The furry bundle pressed his nose to the window. "Meow." The kitten's effort, friendly and calm, signaled a peaceful house.

With a heavy sigh of relief, he stuffed his weapon back in place, opened the door and proceeded forward.

"Hey, buddy." Stooping to rub McTavish behind his ears, Tony was rewarded with another mew and soft purr. "Let's go surprise the lady of the house."

He tiptoed down the hall to the master bedroom and stopped short when he viewed the fully made and empty bed. *What the hell?* He glanced in the bathroom. Cosmetics and bath supplies filled the counter top. He'd never done an inventory but there weren't any obvious holes in the placement. He swung his attention to the walk-in closet. Clothes hung in groups of shirts, sweaters and jackets. *Normal.* His gut wrenched.

Too normal.

If she'd been taken, the abductors wouldn't pack a bag, but Sierra wouldn't go without a fight and there was no sign of a struggle. Accustomed to dealing with surprise situations and trained to remain detached, and without emotion, Tony struggled to keep his pulse even. No way he could remain aloof where Sierra was concerned. His knees folded as he sank onto the edge of the bed and inhaled a deep breath. He needed to think through this scenario and review all the details. The one constant was McTavish, weaving back and forth, with an occasional head-butt to his arm. *He's acting like everything's okay.*

Tony stood and made a beeline for the kitchen. If Sierra left of her own accord, she would have made certain the kitten had ample food and water. He subconsciously held his breath as he re-entered the kitchen. An automatic water dispenser, full, and two bowls of dry pellets sat on a placemat near the door. He exhaled. Disappointed he didn't get a chance to hash things out but certain she was okay; he locked the door and stowed the key back in the metal turtle.

****

Good thing lack of sleep didn't hamper Tony's ability to function. In his basic SEAL training, after completing Hell Week on five hours of sleep, he learned anything could be accomplished if he wanted it bad enough. Tony rolled out of bed and scrubbed both hands up and down his face. The clock blinked six a.m. After he brewed coffee strong enough to float a horseshoe, he'd text Ariel. An early riser, she'd be in the barn, reviewing charts, performing examinations and she'd have knowledge of Sierra's whereabouts last night. Those two were like co-joined twins. If things hadn't been so strange on the last phone call with Sierra, like Twilight Zone strange, he'd text her and ask for the straight up scoop on what the heck was happening, but he didn't want to risk any more fall-out.

A light knock on the outer door jolted Tony out of his introspection. He eased back the curtains and Candi hugged the second step in her cut-offs and bare midriff. *Most likely wants her car keys.* He dropped the fabric and scooped the key ring off the dinette top. The cool breeze between his bare legs reminded him to grab a pair of shorts. Naked was the way he preferred to sleep but not the kind of message he wanted to convey to Miss Candi Pants.

He shoved open the door and greeted her with a smile. "Good morning." He dangled the keys on his index finger. "Looking for these?"

Candi wetted her lips as her eyes fixed on his naked chest. Silence. *That's new.* He grasped her hand and deposited the keys in her palm. "Thanks for the loaner. Work out in the big top in thirty." He enunciated each word then hesitated until she nodded like a bobble head, stumbled backwards off the stairs, and headed toward the exercise tent.

Lordy, he missed Sierra.

Chapter Twenty

"I'm so glad you're spending the night. You had me worried, Sierra. How are you feeling?" Ariel asked, her brown eyes widened, crimping her forehead.

That's the million-dollar question. "Better."

"Have you seen the doctor yet?"

"No, but I've scheduled an appointment for tomorrow."

"Good. Maybe he can give you something for the nausea."

Maybe he can recommend a how-to book for a single mother. "I'm sure he can and will."

"Maybe a dumb question but are you hungry at all? I can heat some chicken noodle soup or fix toasted cheese sandwiches."

"Pizza."

"What?" Ariel asked, an expression of disbelief on her face.

"How about a vegetarian pizza?"

"Uh, okay. We can get it delivered but it might take a while to get out here. I'll slice some veggies to tide us over. Do you feel like a glass of wine?"

Sierra shook her head. *No, no, no.* She squeezed her eyes shut to halt the flow of tears. Unable to stem the steady flow she plunked her bottom on a nearby bench, placed her face in her hands and sobbed.

Ariel kneeled in front of her. "What in the world is

going on?" She brushed strands of hair from Sierra's face. "You can tell me. Is it Tony?"

"Possibly. Almost certainly."

"What the heck did he do?"

"We. What we did."

Ariel placed her hands along Sierra's arms. "You're not making any sense."

Sierra grabbed her purse and fumbled around for a few seconds until she located the small piece of plastic. Lifting it by the end like the tail of a dead mouse, she dangled the test tube like device in front of Ariel's face before laying it on the table. "My test was positive."

Ariel shrieked. "A pregnancy test? Positive? How? Never mind. When?"

Sierra raised an eyebrow and matched Ariel's stare. "While you, Gavin, and Pudge drove into Gainesville for pizza, Tony and I went for a swim. One thing led to another and we had unprotected sex." She observed Ariel's stark surprise, her mouth forming a perfect O while her eyes bugged out.

"I know, I know. It was reckless, and I should've been thinking but I wasn't. I was simply feeling. So, here we are now."

"What are you planning to do?"

"Duh, I'm having the baby." She pointed to her stomach. "Children have always been in my life plan. Preferably bundled with a husband but either way, I'm having this kid."

"Of course, you are. I'm happy hearing you say the words out loud. Does Tony know?"

"No. I haven't found the right time to tell him, if there is a right time. What if he blows up and calls me a slut? And the most dreaded would be, if he'd want to marry me out of obligation?" Sierra fell into Ariel's hug, tears flowing, wetting the front of her T-shirt.

"Tony won't have any of those reactions."

Sierra sniffled and wiped her cheeks with her hands. "How can you be so sure?"

"Gavin confided in me and shared Tony's story which I'll partially share with you. His parents were children of the seventies and never married, which by itself doesn't sound so bad. Plenty of couples cohabited back then and still do, but the father's family rejected Tony as illegitimate. They refused to accept him and treated him like a bastard child. His childhood was haphazard and undisciplined. He ran wild in the streets of Santa Monica until he went to live with his father as a teen."

"That's pathetic," Sierra said. She stood and paced biting the cuticle of her index finger.

"I agree they're pathetic for treating a child in such a reckless way, but the story doesn't end there."

Sierra interrupted. "I know. Tony told me most of the story, the night you guys went into town for pizza. I guess his trust in me is solid."

"You can say that again. Not even the other guys Tony served with know his whole story."

"Gosh, his dad dying of AIDS must have been horrible for him to deal with as a young man." Sierra said as confirmation.

"Yes, he's had a rough childhood but there's a happy ending which affects you."

"What?"

"The happy ending is he joined the Navy and became a SEAL. He understands the beauty of a family and cherishes his brothers. The last thing he'd do is abandon you and his baby. Not going to happen, my friend."

Sierra wiped her eyes and blew her nose. "I've resisted telling him I love him, but I do."

"Tell him how you feel, Sierra. He needs to know."

Sierra rubbed her belly. "First, we get this home test confirmed by a doctor and then I'll tell him."

"Yes. The sooner the better. I'll go with you."

Sierra sniffled back the next round of sobs. "I'm attending a Master Class in Richmond, Virginia in a few weeks. The circus is due there at the same time. I'll surprise him and give him the good news, I hope it'll be good news, but whatever the outcome and whatever his reaction, I'll raise this baby with all the love and protection possible."

Chapter Twenty-One

Richmond, Virginia was the sixth city in as many weeks for the circus and the first time she'd be face to face with Tony. After many long nights of internal debate, she'd resolved to share her "p" news with a surprise visit. The Master Class, scheduled for this evening in downtown Richmond offered the perfect excuse to drop by without appearing to be motivated by expectations of financial support or even marriage. She did, however; feel obligated to disclose her condition to him. It was only fair. If the roles were reversed, she'd want the same forthrightness.

Somewhere deep in her heart she wished for him to be ecstatic upon hearing the news, scoop her up in his arms and devour her mouth and face with kisses but reality screamed, "not going to happen." She realized from previous conversations with Gavin, Tony had been a loner most of his life and the closest thing to family he'd ever experienced were the SEAL Teams.

Her stomach twisted and gurgled as she arrived at the sprawling circus grounds right before noon. Not sure if the morning scourge had returned or her nerves were frayed, she pressed forward to a group of clowns packed into a bright blue Volkswagen Bug. Bile crawled up her throat. She swallowed hard. Twice.

"Excuse me, would you point out the equestrian tent?" She directed her question to the driver wearing a pink wig, rouged cheeks and a polka dot cloth collar. His exaggerated smile, as he gave her directions, didn't seem genuine and gave her the creeps but she understood the illusion of makeup.

"Steady," she told herself and lifted her shoulders as she changed her gait to a determined pace in the direction of a large red and white tent sandwiched between two smaller ones. With a quick circular rub to her stomach, in a comforting motion as a reminder she wasn't alone, she advanced into the dim light and blinked. The pungent aroma of pine-based sawdust shot up her nostrils as if she'd snorted the household cleaner. She screwed up her nose to accommodate the tingling sensation but couldn't stop the explosive sneeze. A startled whinny pierced the air. Jerking her head in the direction of the sound, she blinked again to focus. The vision would stay glued in her brain forever.

A dark horse galloped by sans his rider, kicking up the sawdust. One of the female equestrian acrobats, who resembled an ad for a fitness clothing line, lay sprawled in Tony's arms, head thrown back, batting her eyelashes with one arm around his neck as he cradled her. Her focus darted to Tony. Was he returning the flirtation? With his back toward her, she couldn't tell.

She sneezed again and Tony spun. When he spotted Sierra, he eased the woman to the ground and with a dumfounded expression on his face, waved. With a flash of sequins and long blonde pigtails, the woman kissed his cheek. "That was close. Great catch, Tony."

Sierra did an abrupt about face. Right this minute she couldn't handle the truth. She couldn't cope with what he might say or stomach a lame explanation. The thought of another woman, specifically one like Miss

Obviously Self-Absorbed, being so accepted into his arms chilled her to the bone but he was a free man. Well, a hunted man and they'd made no agreements as to a proposed future. Her breath caught when he said her name, "Sierra?"

The urge to flee back to Gainesville overwhelmed her. She couldn't tell if the jack hammer vibrations resonating in her body were visible to Tony, but she didn't turn around. Instead, she nodded an acknowledgment and briskly rubbed her arms, hoping he didn't notice her shaking hands. *God, I'm such an idiot*. Her inner voice screamed the word. *Idiot. Idiot.* The warmth of a familiar hand squeezed the top of her shoulder and swiveled her around.

A broad smile creased his face. "Hey, baby. What a welcome surprise."

She wanted to strike out, but her tongue lodged between her teeth. *Keep it together, Sierra.* Instead, she retreated a few steps and with a phony, plastered-on smile asked, "Did I interrupt something?" She instantly regretted the degree of resentment in her voice. *This isn't me.*

Tony blanched as if slapped. "Of course not. Never." He strode forward, closing the gap. "Candi and I were practicing the choreo for tonight's performance. A sudden sneeze spooked her horse and she got tossed." He touched her arm. "Lucky I happened to be there."

Likely story. She steeled herself against the emotional rapids, which had possessed her and submitted to his offered embrace. Her mind raced as the hug continued. *Should I believe him? He seems totally sincere.* He rubbed her back in slow, easy circles. *God, I want to believe him.*

To hide her jealousy and protect her tinderbox emotions, she adopted a casual demeanor. Leaning backward, she gazed up into his eyes and said, "I drove here yesterday to attend a Zumba Master Class. Seemed convenient to see you while I'm in the city."

"You arrived yesterday?"

She nodded, uncomfortable as he searched her face. She couldn't speak.

"Got it." Tony winced. "Well, I'm glad you stopped." He dropped his arms. "How's McTavish?"

Crossroads event. Tell him about the baby and chance rejection, anger or worse. Don't tell him and...continue looking more and more like a pumpkin. "He is a feline spark plug. I do appreciate you giving him to me." Her shoulders relaxed and her tone softened.

"Where are you staying? There's room here...with me," Tony said, sticking both hands into the pockets of his pants. "If you want."

Her face heated up and her eyes filled. "Thanks for the offer but I'm staying with a few of the other instructors at a local hotel. Then, I'm headed back tomorrow."

"Oh." His earnest expression mimicked a child whose stocking was empty on Christmas morning.

"Are you free for lunch?" she asked, her resolve to push him away weakened.

His face brightened. "Yes, and I'll fix something tasty and show you my digs. Remember, I'm a hell of a cook." He wrapped his arm around her, hugging her close, as he steered her toward his trailer.

His sweet interest tugged at her heart. She couldn't refuse. With a level head she realized how easy it would be to misread the scene she stumbled onto. His happiness at seeing her was obvious and despite everything, contentment bloomed when she was near him. Besides, a little Italian pasta never hurt anyone or any two.

****

"That was a long trip from Gainesville to Richmond." He brushed her arm with his fingertips. "You feel okay?"

"Sure. Several of the other instructors rode with me and helped drive. Why?"

"You didn't do the usual wolfing down of my pasta."

"Are you saying I eat too much?" Her voice rose as she answered.

"No, baby." He leaned toward her and grabbed her hand. "You just seem preoccupied, less talkative."

Her bottom lip quivered. "So you're saying I talk too much."

"Sierra, I understand the past few weeks have been hard on you but—"

"You have no idea, Tony. None." She pushed back from the table, grinding her chair across the floor, and stood, her hands fisted by her sides."

"Whoa. What's going on?"

She pursed her lips. "Nothing."

"You can tell me anything, sweetie."

She shook her head. "Leave it alone Tony."

His stomach dropped to his ankles. "If there's someone else you need to tell me. Right now."

Lines creased her forehead. "Where did the doubt come from?" She heaved a deep sigh. "Jealousy doesn't become you and there's no reason for it."

He flipped his hands, palms out. "What then?"

"I can't talk about it yet, but I promise I'll tell you." Tears welled in her eyes and threatened to spill down her golden cheeks. "I have to go."

Tony decided to back off despite a gut filled with consternation. "Okay. I trust you."

With her hand on the doorknob, she flashed him a smile, "Good. You should." She opened the door and gingerly descended the flight of stairs before calling out over her shoulder, "I'm going to have a short visit with my uncle before I go."

Tony called out, "Sierra?"

She made an about face, eyes wide, "Yes?"

He followed her and stood close. "I care. I…if you need me, I'm here."

Her lips pressed into a half-smile. "Okay."

She was withholding something, but he didn't pursue it. Instead he asked, "One request?"

"Sure." Her faced relaxed. "What?"

"Text or call me when you arrive home safely."

"No problem. I'm headed back tomorrow. It'll be late, but I'll call."

He extended his arms. "Late doesn't matter."

She accepted his embrace and wrapped her arms around his back, laying her full head of bouncy dark hair on his chest. The heady fragrance of jasmine attacked his senses. His heart raced at the closeness and desire surged in his groin. The urge to collect her in his arms and hurry back up the stairs swamped him. Using his limbs like a shovel, he swept her legs into the curve of his elbow. She reacted by swinging one arm around his neck for balance. "Tony. What the…."

He interrupted her. "Sierra, we…" but stopped

mid-sentence when Alex, his head lowered in concentration, bustled around the corner.

A few feet short of bumping into them, he raised his head and skidded to an abrupt halt. "*Que! Ques es esto, hombre?*"

"Hi, Uncle Alex." Sierra giggled, red-faced, but kept her arm draped around Tony's neck.

Tony maintained his grip, cradling her body while he scrambled for a translation of what Alex said. *Was he in trouble? With the man? Or was it, I'm the man for seducing your niece? No, probably not.* Awkward silence. *Say something clever and charming before you get sucker punched by the protective uncle.*

"Alex," he said with a nod.

The older man slapped Tony on the shoulder and laughed. "Our version of joking. A little American slang, you know?"

No, he didn't know but guessed the "hombre" inferred a generic "man," and not a reference to his manhood being in overdrive. Tony smiled in response. "Whew."

Still smiling, Alex pinched his niece's cheek. "Chuckles, one of the clowns, told me you were here so I came to find you."

He chortled as Tony released Sierra and placed her feet on the ground with care. "But I had no idea this is where I'd find you or who I'd find you with."

"I was just leaving to come find you, Uncle." She glanced at Tony. "We finished our talk."

"Did we?" Tony asked.

Alex said, "Uh-huh. I see." He glanced from Sierra to Tony and back to Sierra where he landed a hard stare before continuing, "I'll give you two privacy to wrap up your conversation. Then, Tony, I could use your help with tonight's act." He smoothed back his jet-black hair before pulling his baseball cap out of his back pocket and positioning it on his head. With a final wink at his niece, he broke into a fast trot toward the middle tent.

Tony's head buzzed as he struggled with what to say because they sure as hell had more to discuss. They hadn't broken eye contact since his last question, but a trembling lower lip now accompanied what had been a confident stare. *Damn-it.* He didn't want to intimidate her. If she would only tell him what's going on, maybe he could help.

Softening his voice, he touched her bottom lip. "Whatever it is, we'll face it together."

She swallowed hard and nodded before placing the palm of her hand over his heart. Then still facing him, she backed up and mouthed, "Soon."

He mouthed back, "Call me." The desire to stop her from leaving burned hot in his chest. But will power, a lesson well learned as a SEAL, overrode the clawing urge and as much as it pained him to back off, he allowed her retreat before speed-walking toward the equestrian tent.

Chapter Twenty-Two

The Zumba event progressed into a raucous, over the top celebration, as usual. Wine appeared along with several other libations. Music blared. The group of bodies performed as one entity with slight variations in jiggle, forward and back, sliding in a sidestep to the left and then to the right. Sierra smiled as she remembered some of the funny quips exchanged between her fellow instructors as they filmed sessions for several promotional social media videos.

Both the music and dance distracted her from the constant roils of her stomach; for the first time in weeks, she didn't feel preoccupied by nausea. The ride home, with her friend's insistence they drive, allowed her needed time to mull over her visit with Tony and evaluate their relationship.

Holy smokes. It's solid. Intact. He told me he cared about me and in my heart, I know it's true. I trust his feelings. I trust him.

Whatever she thought occurred in the center ring had doubtless been assisted by her hormonal overload. Then why hadn't she shared the news with Tony? The perfect opportunity to hash out all the details like, *oh by the way, you're going to be a father* and she blew the chance. For the time being. The fact Tony's assassins still hadn't been located and neutralized worried her wits into a free fall. If she told him, he'd insist on being with her and she couldn't risk his safety. Not now. She'd made a similar mistake as a young girl and the cost was her mother's life but God, she needed him close; she needed him now.

The house was dark when she pulled into the driveway sometime after midnight. *Didn't I leave the front porch light on?* She parked the car and hustled around back, where a bulb monitored by motion detection usually illuminated the back door but as she passed in front of the sensor, nothing happened. *I need to check the fuse box.* Excited at the prospect of holding McTavish and the sound of his steady thrum when she stroked him, she stuck the key in the door lock. But as she rotated her wrist, the door swung open. She gasped.

Did I forget to lock the house when I left? No way. She pulled the key from the lock and hesitated before stepping over the threshold. *I need to make sure McTavish is okay.*

"McTavish? Tavi? Where are you, buddy?" She whispered. *Not a peep but I smell urine, like he sprayed.* Her chest tightened, and her head started to pound. She lifted the switch next to the door and fluorescent light flooded the room.

Thank goodness, the power isn't out.

McTavish scurried from the recesses of the pantry yowling a frantic, "Meow, meow, meow."

His head down, he dashed straight for her legs and rubbed against them. She scooped him into her arms and snuggled him close to her breast, stroking his head and scratching the offered chin. His chest rumbled.

"You okay?" She dipped her nose into his soft fur.

"Thrum. Thrum." With the kitten propped over her shoulder, she closed and dead bolted the door. *Maybe I should call the police. And tell them what? I left my door unlocked.*

She scanned the room; nothing appeared out of place or missing in the kitchen. A set of knives on the counter caught her attention. She plunked the kitten on the floor and withdrew a long, filet knife from the wood block. The salesman warned her about the sharpness of the blade and claimed it could cut off a finger in one slice. Gripping the contoured handle, she started down the hallway, flipping the light switch as she advanced, but stopped short of turning into her bedroom.

Call it gut wrench intuition or simply spooked by the door being unlocked, she decided to check the stone turtle resting in the potted plant by the door where she stored an extra house key. If the turtle top was intact, no one had discovered her secret hiding place and she had most likely, in her rush to leave, locked the door but failed to close it all the way.

"Tavi, you stay inside." She cracked open the door and slipped through onto the cedar-stained wood deck covered in colorful ceramic potted plants. She zeroed in on one container, filled with a blooming hot pink Hibiscus and froze. The top of the turtle was askew. The key remained in place, but the top wasn't flush with the bottom.

She shivered in the humid Florida night while her mind raced. A chill tingled down her back passing an area between her shoulder blades that itched whenever she stressed. With a clawing burn like poison ivy, the spot begged the attention of her Chinese back scratcher. She grabbed the key from the turtle and lurched for the door, retreating inside after securing the deadbolt. Breathing hard gasps, she punched in Ariel's number in a desperate need for her friend to answer despite the late hour.

"Hey, Mamma," a sleepy sounding Ariel asked. "How was your event?"

Ignoring the question, Sierra whispered in staccato beats. "Door. Open. Top of turtle. Off.

"Sierra, you're not making sense. What's going on? Are you hurt?"

"No. Not hurt. Scared speechless. I think someone broke into my house."

"Oh my God! Are you okay? Is McTavish okay? Is anything missing?"

"Tavi is fine. He apparently hid in the pantry. I haven't searched the house yet, but nothing seems out of place."

"Wait a minute. You're currently in the house?"

She dry-swallowed over a lump as her mind spun. "Yes, in the kitchen."

"Sierra, for Christ's sake, grab the kitten and get out. The intruders could still be there, hiding. Stay on the phone with me while you go to your car."

Her knees buckled when she bent to retrieve McTavish and hit the floor. "Where am I going to go?"

"You're driving straight here to the farm."

"What about my things?"

"I'll send Gavin and Pudge over to check out the place as soon as you're here. They can pick up some of your clothes and other necessities then."

Sierra held tight to McTavish, grabbed her purse and forced her legs to work as she escaped out the front door and down the sidewalk to the driveway and the safety of her vehicle. "I'm in the car, doors locked, backing out of the driveway."

"Good. Drive safely. Check in with me every five minutes. I'm calling Gavin."

"Ariel?"

"Yes?

"Don't tell Tony about this, please."

"Uh, why? I guarantee he'll want to be in the loop and be pissed as hell at Gavin for not telling him."

"You know why. I don't want anyone else dying because of me."

"I understand the horrible blame you experienced with your mother's death, but guerillas, not you, killed her during your kidnapping. Don't worry my friend, you'll be safe here with us."

"What about Tony?"

"He's a big boy and has friends skilled at taking care of business. He'll be fine."

Headlights flashed in Sierra's rear view mirror as a car roared close to her bumper. "I have company."

"Are you being followed?"

Sierra gripped the wheel with trembling hands. "Maybe." Her eyes darted in the mirror again, but the blinding glare of the headlights prevented her from discerning any detail about the vehicle except the outline of two heads. She pressed her foot on the gas pedal, her heart racing, her breath shallow.

"Stay on the phone with me and exit at the first well-lighted gas station," Ariel said.

"One coming up." Sierra eased up on the gas and exited to the right off I-75. The car behind followed her off the interstate until she barreled into a truck stop parking lot lighted like a baseball stadium for a night game. While she slid into the closest parking spot, her pursuers rolled into the gas station next door. A thirty-something man dressed in jeans and a blue work shirt got out and glanced in her direction. An oversized semi rolled in and jerked to a stop next to her car, providing her with perfect cover. She eased out of the space, maneuvered around the back of the station and gunned the car out to the side road, veering onto the interstate.

"Hey, are you okay?" Ariel's voice pierced the air around Sierra's headset, she'd put on when she got in her car.

She checked her rear view mirror. Only dark road lay behind her. Sierra choked when she tried to answer. "I think so. I'm turning off the interstate onto the county road."

"Good. If someone was following you, it will be next to impossible for anyone to catch you on Marion County country roads. I'm calling Gavin. Ring me when you're five minutes from the gate."

Sierra checked the rear view mirror. No headlights. Nothing visible but the dark outline of old-growth oaks casting deep shadows as she whipped down the narrow highway. Without the fluorescent glow of urban lights obscuring the sky, stars flowered her path with twinkling light and offered a sense of comfort. Almost at the turnoff for the haven of Wildwood Farms, she sighed and began a slow circular, rub of her belly. "Don't worry. I'll keep you safe, little one."

Chapter Twenty-Three

Sierra smiled at the gray bundle sleeping next to her as she turned down the familiar gravel road onto Wildwood Farms. McTavish raised his head at the crunch and vibration of the new surface and uncurled from his nap. She reached over and scratched his head. Peering one final time into the rear view mirror, she observed only black. *No headlights. Whew.* She heaved a sigh and slowed to a crawl until she coasted up to the new security gate.

Installed after Ariel's crazy ex sneaked onto the property and tried to kidnap her, the ten-foot wrought iron barrier served as a deterrent to uninvited guests. Not that anyone on the premises was worried about Mr. Sleaze Bag at the present. He was serving time and her best friend was married to a former commando who wouldn't give a second thought about shortening the life of anyone who dared harm his wife. With the driver's side window rolled down, she pressed the intercom button.

"Hey, why didn't you text me?" Ariel asked. "I would have opened the gate already."

"Sorry. Preoccupied." The gates squeaked as they began to open.

"Glad you're here. Come to the main house. We'll meet you there."

"All right but how did you figure out the buzzer

was me?"

"Pudge has been busy." Ariel chuckled. "He installed camera's all over the property."

Gavin's voice boomed into the intercom, "I put my foot down about having surveillance in the bedrooms and bathrooms, especially our bedroom."

Sierra giggled. "On my way, you two." She released the button and eased her car through the opened gate. A clunk signaled the infrared sensor had automatically closed and relocked the entrance. A wave of relief washed over her as she held down the window button. She swiped at her eyes as tears threatened to spill down her cheeks.

All her life, she'd taken the safety and freedoms of living in America for granted but with the violation of her own personal space, she recognized the boundary of Wildwood Farms existed as her perimeter of safety and freedom: at least, for the immediate future.

Unable to withhold the pent-up emotion of the past few days, sobs lifted her chest in choppy breaths. She steered the car between two of the one-hundred-year-old oak trees, lining the long, winding entrance and braked to a quiet stop. She shut off the headlights. With both hands folded on top of the steering wheel, she dipped her forehead and let a torrent of tears fall.

****

Gavin opened the front door and with one arm braced on the doorjamb and leaned out. "Has Sierra arrived at the farm, yet?" he asked.

Ariel sat on the edge of the double porch swing and shuffled her feet back and forth. "No." She frowned and clutched the chain. "She's had plenty of time to get here. I'm worried."

He hopped onto the porch letting the door slam shut. Ariel jumped. "Sorry babe." He squeezed her shoulder. "I'll grab my rifle and my LED flashlight. You stay here in case she swung around the back and entered by the barn."

"Be careful."

"Always am." He grabbed her chin and kissed her on the lips. "Pudge is in the kitchen."

Gavin disappeared into the house and returned within minutes with an AR-15 and a small black flashlight fitted onto a rail on top of the gun's barrel. He hopped off the porch and climbed into his pickup as the glare of oncoming headlights brightened the final turn on the long driveway to the main house. Glancing out the back window he observed Pudge on the porch beside Ariel, also armed. As the car rolled closer, they all recognized Sierra's BMW and smiled and waved like she was arriving to attend a Sunday picnic.

Ariel and Pudge joined him in the driveway, waving and smiling their fake, everything's lovely, faces also.

After she stopped the car, Gavin opened the door. "Need help with anything?"

"I only have my purse and McTavish and the clothes on my back." Using her index finger, she flicked away a lone tear poised at the outer corner of her eye.

"Pudge and I will go to your house and pick up whatever you need." Gavin directed his attention to his friend. "No going through her lingerie drawer."

Ariel hugged her friend and petted McTavish. "I'm tucking you two away in the guest bedroom of the main house." Ariel tugged her friend toward the front door.

"Gavin, give me about thirty minutes and I'll bring you a list of the things she needs."

He nodded with a grin, "I'm timing you."

Right on time, Ariel reappeared on the front porch, a piece of paper in her hand.

"Here's a list." She thrust it in his hand and peered around the porch. "Where's Pudge?"

"Packing a few things for the trip to Sierra's."

She shook her head. "Don't need to know. Don't want to know."

Gavin chuckled then perused the list. "How's she doing?"

"She's shaken up as might be expected but she and the bab…. Damn it. She's fine."

His head jerked up. "Wait a minute, what?"

"What do you mean what?" Her eyes widened. "She and McTavish are fine and sound asleep."

"Ariel." He raised an eyebrow and made a rolling motion with one hand. "You started to say something. Spit it out."

She broke eye contact and shook her head.

"What gives?"

"I've been sworn to secrecy, Gav."

"And our agreement on the subject of secrets is what…?"

"We don't keep secrets from each other." She rolled her eyes. "But I promised."

Pudge appeared, arms loaded, ready for covert warfare. Gavin nodded to him. "Okay. I gotta go but we'll discuss this after I get home from Sierra's."

She pinched the bridge of her nose. "Be careful, Gavin. These guys are dangerous."

"Baby, I'm in my element here. Remember, I used

to hunt enemy combatants for a living."

"Oh, I remember. Sleepless nights, floor pacing, hand wringing and praying a government car didn't pull up in the driveway."

He pulled her into a tight embrace and gave her what he hoped was a reassuring kiss. "I'll be fine."

She peered up at him and said, "See you when you get home."

Chapter Twenty-Four

Tony paced between the circus tents, head bowed, clutching his burner phone to his ear while he simultaneously stuck his index finger in his other ear. He needed to concentrate, and the cacophony of circus sounds made privacy difficult. With a silent command, he willed Gavin to answer his call. *Voice mail. Shit.*

After listening to Gavin's brief message, he left one of his own, "Hey asshole, call me."

Worry wasn't something he spent a lot of time on, but no word from Sierra in the two days since her surprise visit concerned him. He'd called her and left what he hoped was a light-hearted, casual message, "Hey, checking in. Haven't heard from you. Give me a shout." She'd promised to text or call him when she arrived home but didn't. Something was wrong.

Frustrated by his inability to control the situation, Tony stuffed the phone in the zippered pocket of his shorts, then jogged toward the fence line of the fairground's property. The sawdust smell of the circus receded behind him, replaced with the floral perfume from the multitude of blooming wildflowers. The gloom of twilight spread and soon, only the ambient light from the circus guided his path. Running helped intensify his focus but this time a knot of dread, sick and hard, persisted in his stomach, forcing him into a faster pace despite the hot, humid air. Sweat poured down his face and drenched his T-shirt as his pumped his arms back and forth in perfect balance to the pound of his tennis shoes on the hard dirt surface. Without any cover and exposed, he squinted toward the thick tree line on the other side of the enclosure. The dense forest provided a multitude of hiding places for someone hell-bent on collecting a bounty. As he picked up his speed, subtle undertones of rotting matter from the forest floor drifted across his path.

A sudden breeze rolled through the tall, untended grass next to the chain link fence. The wild stalks bent in waves. The loud snap of a branch arrested his attention. He skidded to a stop. Was the grass moving from the wind or against the wind like someone stealing through it? *Christ. I'm acting paranoid. Enough hiding.* He clenched his fists and spat. *I can't live like this any longer. It isn't me.*

Breaking into a sprint, he circled the farthest corner of the enclosure. Without slowing his pace, Tony reversed direction, and with his eyes locked onto the distant banners waving atop the lighted tent poles, he took flight. The shadowy landscape blurred as he sped past. Freed by his decision, the worry and frustration, like the weight of a ships' anchor, lifted. He didn't want to leave Alex in a lurch but after he fessed up, about having hot sex with the man's beloved niece, he'd most likely be ordered off the property.

Either way, he was out of here.

Chapter Twenty-Five

Driving was Gavin's guilty pleasure and all the team guys fully and completely understood that, so when he climbed behind the steering wheel, he didn't expect any argument from Pudge. And he didn't get any. Pudge was already headed for the shotgun position before Gavin pulled out the key fob from his pocket.

Once a team operated together for a period of months, the mind-sync automatically occurred. It was one of things that made SEALS effective at their jobs. Another was being accustomed to silence. No one experienced discomfort with quiet. So, for most of the fifty-minute drive to Gainesville and Sierra's house, both men contemplated their own thoughts and the back of their eyelids.

During the final stretch, as if the question burned in his brain from the first block, Pudge asked, "Hey, what was all the noise about? You and Ariel weren't fighting, were you?"

"Fighting? No. We were *discussing*," Gavin said.

"Discussing what, if I might ask?" Pudge cocked his eyebrow in response to Gavin's death glare.

"Whatever is going on with Sierra, you cheeky bastard."

"And what might that be?"

"Whatever it is, Ariel's been sworn to secrecy."

Pudge waggled one brow. "Maybe she's prego?"

Gavin swerved the wheel and hit the curb with a hard thud. "Holy hell." As he righted the truck, Pudge used his fingers and counted the number of weeks since Tony and Sierra had stayed behind at the farm while they drove into town for pizza. He held up eight digits.

"Double holy hell. I wonder if Tony knows?" Gavin rubbed his eyes like he'd miscounted the number of fingers.

"Doubt it. Pretty sure he'd be here if he knew." Pudge nodded his head, then asked, "You sure it's Tony's?"

"If she's pregnant, Tony's the daddy. Sierra's all about family. Zumba is her family. Ariel and I are her family. Alex is her family…."

Pudge interrupted, "I get it." He shifted his shoulders. "Tony has a right to know, man."

"Agreed." He glanced at Pudge. "Once I verify, she is, in fact, expecting, I'll tell him."

"What if Ariel makes you promise not to say anything?"

Gavin winked. "Then, over to you."

"He'll be pissed if he thinks we held out on him."

"So, we won't hold out," Gavin responded as they pulled onto Sierra's street.

"I hear you brother," Pudge said.

Gavin put the truck in park a few houses away and brought his cell phone to eye level. One missed call from Tony. "Speak of the devil." He flipped the phone around, so Pudge could view the screen.

Pudge's eyes widened.

"I should listen to the message before we go in," Gavin said as he punched the voice mail icon. His lips thinned into a broad smile, creasing the lines around his eyes before he pressed replay and handed the phone to Pudge.

"Sounds angry," Pudge said, returning the phone. "Cabin fever or something more urgent?"

"Your guess is as good as mine, but he can simmer while we check out the house. We need to get in there. I'll call him on the way home." Gavin changed the ring mode to vibrate and slipped the phone back in the belt holster before he pressed down on the handle and pushed open the truck door. "I doubt if anyone would stick around after they broke into the house, but we should use precaution."

"Agreed but if she interrupted them before they finished searching for whatever they wanted…." Pudge let Gavin fill in the blanks.

Gavin nodded and pointed the tactical flashlight beam into the woods across the street as they walked, illuminating the area with the intensity of a police spotlight. They stopped in front of Sierra's house.

"Strange. No lights." Gavin spoke out of the side of his mouth but loud enough for Pudge to hear. "Didn't Sierra say she left a hall light on?" He switched off his flashlight and his hand slid to the concealed side arm tucked in his waist band.

Pudge nodded. "Might not be able to see it from here if the blinds are closed. We need to get closer. Go left behind the grove of trees. I'll cover you."

Gavin crouched and crabbed sideways across the corner of the yard until he reached the tree line, his gun drawn and pointed toward the house. Once behind the massive grove of live oaks, he hand-signaled for Pudge to stay alert and circle right, then continued left to the back of the house. As he rounded the corner, Pudge propped his leg on the back-porch step, grinned and tapped the crystal on his watch band.

Gavin tucked his 9mm in his belt and saluted the sarcasm with his middle finger. "Feels like we're the only ones here," he whispered, "but before we go inside to fill Sierra's shopping list, I'm calling her." He pointed to the amber light above the back door. "This one wasn't on?"

Pudge said, "Appears to be a motion sensor but it didn't turn on when I neared the porch."

"Got it." He peered inside the window. "Well, the hall light appears to be on. I want to confirm what she remembers about how she left the house."

"Good idea. We might be chasing ghosts."

"Or not." Gavin withdrew his phone from the leather phone case threaded on his belt and scrolled through his contact list. He adjusted his Blue-tooth head set and tapped the green phone symbol.

"Dude, you have Sierra's phone number on speed dial?" Pudge raised his left eyebrow.

"Not speed dial." He rolled his eyes. "But she's in my contacts with a star next to her name because she almost always knows where my wife is." In a playful gesture, Gavin laid his palm on Pudge's chest and pushed him. "Speed dial," he huffed.

Pudge chuckled as he pointed in the direction of the truck. "Getting my toolbox to set up security on this place." Before Gavin could respond, he ducked around the corner.

"Are you at the house?" Sierra asked, a little breathless. "Is everything okay?"

Gavin refocused his attention to the phone screen. "We're here. Everything appears okay from the outside.

We haven't gone in yet. I have a few questions."

"Sure."

"Did you leave lights on in the house or outside when you left to go to the farm?"

"Yes, the kitchen and hall lights."

Gavin clenched his jaw as he peered into the dark kitchen. "What about the front porch?"

"That's the thing, Gavin. I could have sworn I left the light on, but the front was dark when I arrived home." Her voice wobbled. "And the top on the turtle, where I hide my extra key, was askew." She inhaled a shaky breath. "And the door was unlocked."

Gavin glanced at the turtle. *Top off, empty*. "Did you take the hidden key with you?"

"Yes. I have the key. Why?"

"No reason other than I noticed it missing." Gavin nodded to Pudge when he came around the corner. "Pudge is going to work his magic to keep you and your property secure and then we'll retrieve the items on your list."

"Thank him for me."

"Will do." Gavin disconnected the call and stowed his phone in the case. He pulled his weapon and motioned to Pudge they were entering the house. Positioning himself in front, he stretched his left hand and twisted the doorknob, then pressed his foot against the door, swinging it open. He crouched and veered right, shining the beam of his flashlight over the gun's barrel, sweeping the kitchen as Pudge glided in behind him and veered left. He extended the beam into the pantry, checking the back corners. "Clear."

Pudge eased down the short hallway to the living room while Gavin continued toward the back of the house and the two bedrooms. His interest was in the guest room/office where Sierra had a desk and where he hoped she had not stored any information about Tony's whereabouts or the travel route of her uncle's circus.

If common thieves had broken in, they'd be in a hurry and wouldn't care what kind of mess they left behind. The fact that the house was spotless, concerned him.

"Living room is clear." Pudge said as he came in the office. "Nothing out of place."

"That's what worries me," Gavin said.

Pudge nodded he understood. "You want me to check out the other bedroom?"

"Yeah. Go ahead and finish clearing the house." Gavin sifted through the corner pile of papers placed in a neat stack. *Someone is preparing for the bar exam.* A completed application caught his eye. Sierra listed her uncle, Alex, as next of kin and stated his employment as business owner. His address had a suite number and was no doubt one of those faux offices with a rented post office box. *Nothing specific. Smart girl.*

Next, he opened the middle drawer and, no surprise, a neat grouping of pens was bundled in a rubber band next to a package of note cards, a roll of stamps and a few lined, legal pads of paper.

Pudge entered the room and announced, "All clear. We're alone."

Gavin glanced up and said, "Good," as he shoved his arm deep into the drawer. Sliding his fingers along the inside, they brushed against a piece of paper taped to the top. "Bingo!"

His breathing quickened as he peeled off the tape holding the paper in its' hiding place and laid it on the desk. He clicked on the flashlight and gasped as he read the circus travel schedule complete with dates and locations.

"Pudge, we have a SNAFU."

****

Sierra jumped at the sound of a car door. On edge all evening about what the guys might find at her house, she hurried out the front door. Ringing her hands, unable to wait for them to climb onto the porch, before she called out, "Did you find out who broke into my house? Was anything missing?"

Gavin, his expression unreadable, advanced up the steps and retrieved a folded piece of yellow letter-sized paper from his back-jean pocket. He handed it to Sierra and said, "This."

She gasped and clutched the paper to her chest. "How did you…I hid this…where was it?"

"Taped to the underside of the center desk drawer in your office."

With a deep exhale she said, "Right where I left it." She searched Gavin's face for a sign of disapproval at her inadequate spy skills.

Instead, he smiled and indicated for her to step back into the house. He pointed toward the sofa. "You and I need to talk." He glanced over his shoulder as Pudge and Ariel both entered the room and signaled for them to take a seat as well. "We searched and cleared the house, Pudge changed the lock, set up a surveillance system he can monitor from his phone. Nothing was broken or missing, that either of us can tell."

Sierra interrupted, "That's great, right? Maybe it was some teenagers in search of cash for drugs but I don't keep cash in the house."

Gavin nodded. "Which is the problem. The house was searched with meticulous and thorough care."

"How do you know?" Sierra asked.

His eyes steadied first on Sierra, then Ariel. "They picked up items and when they put them back the placement was a slight degree off. The indentation of desk legs on the carpet for one, dust circles on the mantel was another, which indicates they are pros. *Not* teenagers and it's the same MO as Tony's apartment."

Sierra said, "What do you mean same MO as Tony's apartment?"

"His apartment was broken into, but nothing was taken. Everything remained intact, neat as a pin. If he hadn't had his own security set-up he'd never known. Then, his brakes were sabotaged."

Sierra grabbed Ariel's arm for support. "Do you think they found the circus' show schedule?"

Gavin, with a grim twist to his mouth, said, "Don't know. Maybe not. I think you interrupted their search."

Sierra gasped. "Could they have been in the house when I came home?"

His tight gaze seemed to bore holes straight through her. "It's possible."

Instinctively, she palmed her stomach and rubbed. "Oh my God."

Gavin said, "We're on full alert, people. Sierra, you're staying here until we find these thugs. Pudge, we need to warn Tony."

"Agreed," Pudge said. "You gonna call him?"

"Right after Ariel and I have a private conversation." He stood and offered his wife a hand.

Sierra's gut clenched. The gig was up.

Chapter Twenty-Six

Tony, mind set on what he had to do, poured on the speed for the return run back to the circus grounds. His leg muscles burned but the tenseness in his shoulders had disappeared and his mind cleared of the constant 'what next, what next' that had haunted his thoughts.

With his breathing labored after the intense physical exertion, he slowed to a brisk walk as he entered the grouping of tents and trailers. A flashing red light drew his attention.

An ambulance rolled to a stop outside the equine practice tent. He transitioned into a jog. Two men dressed in basic blue and white uniforms leaped out of the front doors. The driver, being waved forward by one of the male trick riders, sped into the tent carrying a large black bag, while the second man opened the rear doors and pulled out a collapsible stretcher.

A crowd of circus workers gathered around the tent opening and spoke in low whispers. As he approached, someone grabbed his arm hard enough to halt him. Caught by surprise, he whirled around, arm raised, and fist balled and ready.

"Whoa, easy," Alex said. "I've been looking for you. I knocked on your trailer, but you didn't answer." His normally tanned skin appeared pale, his face drawn in a tight frown.

Tony relaxed. "I took a run. What happened?"

"It's Candi. She's hurt."

"How bad?"

"Not sure. One of the other trick riders found her in the sawdust, unconscious, so I called the ambulance."

Tony shoved through the onlookers and raced to the center of the ring where the EMT positioned two fingers on Candi's neck. He dropped to his knees but stayed silent until the technician released his position and pulled out a small flashlight. "What's her pulse?" Tony asked.

"Who are you?" the tech queried as he lifted one of Candi's eyelids and shined a small light across her eyeball without a glance in Tony's direction.

"I'm her boss and a trauma nurse practitioner," Tony answered. Since the guy didn't flinch Tony figured he was unimpressed with his creds.

"Steady at sixty-two," he replied.

"Other vitals?" Tony persisted, an evenness to his voice, despite the continued lack of eye contact. He wanted answers, not compete for the guy's job.

"Normal but eyes appear sensitive to light and could indicate a possible concussion." He glanced over his shoulder and met Tony's eyes for half a minute before returning his attention to Candi. "She needs to go to the E.R. for additional testing and monitoring."

"Agreed," Tony said, "and perfect timing," he added when the second EMT entered the tent and hustled the gurney over to them.

"Help me lift her onto the stretcher," the EMT said to his co-worker as he pressed the lever down sending the bed to the ground. "One, two, three, lift."

With Tony at Candi's head and both EMTs at her legs, they transitioned her from the ground to stretcher in one synchronized effort. One of the EMTs veered off while he spoke into the radio perched on his shoulder while the other one readied the stretcher for the ambulance.

Tony assumed the guy was calling ahead to the hospital, "I'll stay with her until you load her," he said to the EMT across from him,

Alex filled the space left by the emergency technician and asked, "How is she?"

"A possible concussion," Tony answered. "Do you know how or what happened?"

Alex shook his head, "No idea. From what I can gather she was in the tent alone."

"Rule number one. Never practice without a spotter. What could have possessed her to—?"

Alex glanced around at the crowd of curious circus workers and leaned in close to Tony's ear. "From the way she purrs when you're around, I'd say it had something to do with impressing you."

Tony's face reddened and he glared at Alex who obviously trounced on a nerve. "I can assure you I haven't encouraged her." He gazed around at the circle of curiosity-seekers and seethed through his teeth, "Frigging looky-loos."

Alex shouted and waved his arms, "Everybody get back to work. Candi is being taken care of."

As the crowd began to disperse and the two had more privacy, Alex addressed Tony's comment. "No one blames you for her poor judgment."

"I should have made my lack of interest more obvious. I should have told her there's someone, but I didn't want to involve Sierra any more than she's already involved in my messy, chaotic world."

Before Alex could respond, Candi's eyes fluttered open. She squinted as she gazed around as if the light hurt her eyes. "Where am I?" She attempted to sit up and winced from apparent pain. She lay back down.

"You're in the equestrian tent," Tony answered. "Where does it hurt?"

In silence, she pointed to her right side and then to the top of her head. Most likely cracked or bruised ribs and a concussion, he decided. "Does it hurt when you take a deep breath?"

She drew in a breath and yelped. "Yes."

He wanted to chastise her for breaking the rules, but her doe eyes brimmed with tears and he resolved the pain of cracked ribs and a possible concussion was punishment enough. "You're going to be okay, Candi, but lie still. It'll hurt less. The ambulance is here to take you to the hospital."

"Will you go with me?" she asked, a single tear painted a trail down her dusty cheek.

"Sure. I have to ask you," he kept his voice even. "What were you thinking, riding without a spotter?"

Her bottom lip quivered, and she shifted her gaze away from him. "It was supposed to be a surprise. I…I…." She stuttered and then stared into space as if collecting her thoughts. "My memory is fuzzy."

God. I'm such a douche bag. If I hadn't been so concerned about myself, I would have noticed her feelings ran deeper than a high school crush. I would have let her know right from the start…What? I was being hunted by assassins and had a girlfriend stashed in Gainesville or was it now Ocala?

Candi snapped her fingers, interrupting his self-abnegation. "I remember," she said, her mood brighter.

180

"I wanted to impress you with perfecting the back somersault we practiced."

He targeted her with all the frustration boiling in his gut and exploded. "You mean the back flip off a galloping horse I told you was one of the most extreme and dangerous tricks you'd ever attempt?" He leaned in to bring his face closer. "You mean *that* one, missy?"

"I'm sorry." Her expression greened and she clasped her hand over her mouth, right before she sprayed him with vomit.

As Tony flicked the puke off his fingers after wiping his face, the first attendant walked up and gasped at the sight. "What the heck, man?"

"Pay back, I guess," Tony said.

Grinning, the tech handed him a towel. "Pay back for what?"

"Never mind. I'll go clean up and follow you to the hospital.

"You don't need to come," Candi said.

"I want to make sure you get a CT scan and x-rays. Might have a cracked rib." Then, with a smile he said, "I'll need to borrow your car."

She mustered up an okay and told him where she'd left the keys as the EMT wheeled her to the ambulance.

They loaded her into the back of the vehicle before Tony circled toward his trailer. He needed to change clothes because the stench from his sweat-soaked running shorts and white tank top screamed, "Stop, drop and roll…away from him."

All the reasons he'd given himself for leaving the circus evaporated. Why Sierra hadn't called him had to go on the back burner. He'd have to count on the people around her, his friends, to protect her for now. He couldn't leave Alex or Candi, either. She was their star trick rider and she was out of commission for the near future, but the show must go on, as they say. Maybe they could fill in with a seal balancing a ball on his nose. Did they even have a seal act? He'd been so involved in his own problem; he'd omitted sitting through a complete rehearsal.

"Slack bastard," he admonished himself as he stepped into the steam-filled shower stall. The pulsing jet of hot water invigorated him. He stuck his head in the center of the flow and allowed a minute for his mind to clear before he grabbed the large white bar of unscented soap on the nearby shelf. The creamy foam erased the body odor and the cold-water rinse, which followed, took away his tiredness from the long run.

After a quick towel-off he snatched a short-sleeved button-down shirt and cargo shorts from his dresser. The top's fabric hugged his chest and wrapped around his solid biceps. He left the shirt tail out and tucked his junk inside and behind the zipper. He hadn't worn underwear since SEAL training where he learned running on sand wearing skivvies in standard issue Navy shorts meant deep chafes in the crotch.

He readied himself with a final glance in the hall mirror and a quick finger brush through his dark hair before he swung open the trailer door. Alex, fist raised to knock, stumbled back down the stairs.

"I was just heading over to the hospital to get an update on Candi."

"No need," Alex said. "I'll go."

"I think we both know why she broke the rules. I need to make this right."

Alex stiffened. "What you need to do is stay put

and come up with a show, instead of revealing yourself at the hospital."

Tony shook his head. "I'll be careful. I'm going."

"Well, hombre. If you're sleeping with my niece, I think I have a right to say something. If you reveal your whereabouts, it could put her at risk as well."

"I should have told you about Sierra and me."

"Why didn't you?"

"Truth?"

"Yes, the whole truth." Alex rolled his hand and wrist in a forward motion. "Shoot."

"Her reluctance to commit to me or our relationship confused me." Tony frowned. "I know she has feelings for me but there's an emotional barrier I can't penetrate."

"Has she ever talked about her past?" Alex asked. "About her childhood in Colombia?"

"Not really but then I haven't revealed much of my childhood either."

Alex opened his mouth for a couple of seconds, then shut it, clamping his lips. He stared at his shoes, then lifted his gaze heavenly as if in silent prayer. A single tear flowed down his cheek until he swiped it away. "Sierra survived horrendous brutality as a child."

Tony clenched his jaw as his attention snapped onto Alex."What happened?"

"Ever heard *Fuerzas Armadas Revolucionarias de Colombia*, better known as FARC?

"Of course. They call themselves a revolutionary force but they're really a terrorist group. Some of the Team guys worked with the Colombian government to stop their drug smuggling and human…trafficking…" He stuttered the last two words. "No way!"

"When Sierra was eight," Alex explained "she was kidnapped near the village where her parents taught school. Her mother fought the two kidnappers with a hoe but they shot her in the head."

He paused for a long moment before continuing. "They shot her in front of Sierra, then disappeared into the jungle with her. They held her for a year until the military rescued her. Luckily, she wasn't sold into slavery or we might never have found her."

"Christ. I had no idea. Why didn't she tell me?"

"Probably the same reason she stopped receiving counseling."

"And that reason would be?"

"Unless you yourself have been kidnapped by terrorists and held captive for a year in squalid living conditions, how could you possibly understand?"

"I have to ask but not because it affects one damn how I feel about her. Was she raped?"

"No, but another year or two in captivity and one of the scum would have taken her for his own," Alex growled. "She would have been at his mercy, or he would have sold her into slavery.

Tony leaned back. "As a nurse practitioner in a busy E.R., I've dealt with sexual assault survivors plenty of times. I was thinking I might be able to offer…I don't know…something…an empathetic ear?" He heaved a sigh. "Thank God they rescued her."

Alex nodded. "Sierra's the strongest woman I know. After she testified against the group, despite receiving death threats, I arranged asylum for her here in the U.S."

"No wonder she is so afraid of guns."

"Afraid? No way. Bad memories? Yes." Alex

raised his index finger and pointed it at Tony imitating a gun. "They were training her to be a fighter."

"For fuck's sake." The image of Sierra locked and loaded, firing an AK47 contradicted everything he thought he knew about her.

Tony rubbed his forehead. "This whole thing must be terrifying for her." *I hate not being there.* "She's safe with Gavin and Pudge," he said as if convincing himself. With a spin on his heel, he retreated, and barked over his shoulder, "Driving to the hospital. Gonna check on Candi."

"We had an agreement," Alex shouted at his back. "If you expose your location, you could put Sierra in jeopardy."

Tony dragged his sun glasses off his head onto the bridge of his nose without breaking his determined pace toward Candi's car. "I'll be careful."

"You're staying here, mister," Alex spat the word 'here.' He jogged until he matched Tony's stride. "I know you think you're invincible but you're not and neither is Sierra."

He glared at Alex without slowing. "Invincible? You think ego is my motivation?" He shook his head in disbelief. "You got me all wrong."

The older man planted himself in front of Tony and blocked his path. "I know you feel responsible for Candi's accident."

"Correct, *jefe,*" Tony said and maneuvered around Alex who grabbed the younger man's arm as he passed and whirled him around.

The unexpected aggression caught Tony off guard and thrust him sideways, but he quickly regained his balance, and jerked his arm free. With his legs braced a foot apart, he faced Alex, whose dark eyes glistened with heat. The tension sparked between them.

"I feel responsible for Candi getting injured." Tony relaxed his stance. "She was trying to impress me with the trick. Had I told her about my relationship with Sierra, she wouldn't have taken such a risk."

"Maybe, maybe not." Alex rubbed his hands across his face. "Candi is young and a daredevil. She's the one who broke the safety rules."

"I should've told her about my relationship with Sierra," Tony insisted. "I need to follow through and make sure she's okay.

"Seems like you've made your decision." Alex leaned in close enough Tony could smell the spicy green sauce he'd eaten for lunch. "Do what you want but I've made my decision, too." They were toe-to-toe, but Tony decided if Alex swung, he'd duck. Enough was at stake without adding a brawl; one the older man was sure to lose.

"If you insist on putting yourself in harm's way and you leave these grounds…."

Tony interrupted, "You're one stubborn…."

Alex held up his hand indicating he wanted to finish. "Don't come back," he said, over-enunciating the words. His nostrils flared and the finger he pointed, shook. He turned and stalked off.

Tony rolled his eyes as he called out, "C'mon Alex. Don't walk away." He started to follow but halted when his phone rang. *What now?* Tearing it from the case hooked onto his belt, he gaped at the caller ID. *Gavin.* "Bro. I've been trying to reach you."

"Yeah. I know. It's been a little busy around here."

"What's going on?" With thoughts of Alex's

revelation about Sierra still fresh, Tony's temples started to ache. "Is Sierra okay?" In need of privacy, he hurried back toward his trailer.

"She's okay…now, but her space was violated. Her house was searched."

"When? I was just…." He stopped before he spilled the news he'd been spying on Sierra and caught a load of crap for being off the reservation.

"Just what?" Gavin's tone conveyed he appreciated his best friend's impulsive nature all too well.

"When was the break-in?" Tony repeated as he glanced around to make sure he'd traveled out of ear shot of curious circus staff.

"Recent. In the last few days."

"Christ. Was anything taken?"

"Not taken but…." He stopped and changed course. "Were you aware Sierra had a copy of the circus' travel schedule, complete with cities and dates?"

"No." He hesitated. "She did? Where?"

"It was taped under the center desk drawer in her home office."

"And the paper was still there?"

"Yes, but some of the tape was missing. That's how I found it. One corner was hanging down and caught in the drawer when I opened it."

"What are you saying?" He already knew the answer, but he wanted confirmation. He wanted to hear Gavin say it out loud.

"We think the assassins figured out your connection to Sierra, tracked her and found her house. They broke in and searched for evidence of your location. Explains why nothing appears missing."

Tony's head began to pound. "Fuck me. Where is

Sierra right now?"

"Safe at the farm, but we don't know if the tangos found the schedule so sit tight, for now. We'll come get you when we know more."

"I'm through sitting this out, Gavin. I have a situation here I need to take care of before I can get back to Ocala and the farm, but I'm coming."

"Listen, man. I understand how you feel but the one thing keeping you alive also keeps you alone."

"Too late. There's a girl…never mind. Too much to go over on the phone."

Gavin blew out a long audible sigh. "Sierra's pregnant."

A shiver covered Tony's body as his mind swept over their last encounter. It all made sense. "How far along?" He hoped; no, he was certain the baby was his.

"Don't know for sure. Ariel and Sierra, it seems, had a secret pact, but Ariel slipped last night, and half said the word. I pulled the little surprise the rest of the way out. No pun intended."

Tony snorted. "Is Pudge in on this?"

"He's the one who put the time line together and originally figured it out." Gavin's voice deepened as he continued. "It's your baby, Tony, and here you are already shacking up with another woman."

"No. For Pete's sake, no. Candi is one of the trick riders and works for me."

"Candi? Sounds young, blonde and willing. And you're not tapping it?"

"Oh, believe me, the temptation has been laid out like a Sunday picnic, but no."

"Then what's the problem?"

"I didn't tell her about Sierra, is the problem." He

blew out a breath. "I should've but I didn't."

"You were smart not to give anything away about your former life."

"I'm not that noble, man. I think on some level I was probably enjoying the attention."

"Okay, so you're a prick, but a smart one for keeping the situation to yourself."

"Gav, she had a serious accident this morning. I feel responsible. While I was out for a run, she tried a dangerous riding trick without a spotter. That landed her in the hospital. I was on my way to check on her when you called."

"You need to stay there," Gavin said. "Alex can cover her and give you a sit-rep."

Tired of being told what he should and shouldn't do, Tony replied through gritted teeth, "Time for me to get a grip on my own messes." Gavin began a protest, but Tony had already punched the off button.

Within seconds, his phone buzzed again and Gavin's name appeared on the ID. Tony held the off button down until the phone shut off. Pissed at how much the well-ordered life he'd worked so hard to achieve had spiraled out of control, he slammed his fist into the open palm of his other hand. His breathing hitched as hot tears threatened to spill down his cheeks. He swiped at his face and struggled to gain control over the grief threatening to swamp him. Either way he was royally screwed.

If he stayed, he stayed as a man who could no longer live with himself, a man who ran from trouble, and a man who refused to accept responsibility for his actions; a man who relinquished protection of his woman to another and failed Candi, his charge, when she needed him the most. If he left, he torched his bridge with Alex and who knew how the fall-out from that decision would affect his relationship with Sierra. Any slip-ups while he was on the move and he could be putting the lives of everyone he held dear at risk.

Frustration flooded his senses and a feral growl slipped through his gritted teeth as his emotions teetered on a tight rope without a net. In need of release from the see-sawing anger and grief, he gripped the top of his collared shirt and with a powerful yank, ripped the edges apart. A chaos of popped buttons flew in every direction.

Tony peered down at his torn shirt. "Shit." He tugged it off his back, balled up the cloth and tossed it in one of the oversized trash barrels outside his trailer before he stormed inside. The release of anger cleared his mind. *Sierra's pregnant with my baby and now she's in danger*.

The choice was simple. With the focus of a well-trained ambush predator, he mentally ran through the various potential scenarios and a plan formulated.

He knew what he needed to do, and God help anyone who got in his way.

Chapter Twenty-Seven

Sierra sucked in a deep breath as she entered the kitchen of the main house. "What smells so good?"

"I thought you were still napping," Ariel said as she tilted her head and smiled at her friend. With her hand on the stereo knob, she increased the volume. "A little music to cook by."

Arms stretched high over her head, Sierra smiled and moaned. "Such a good sleep." Swaying in rhythm to the pop tune she added, "Umm. Good music choice. Need any help with dinner?"

"Take it easy," Ariel replied. "I got this."

"You know, Bessie Mae maintains her title as first place housekeeper and cook without any runners-up. She roasted a pork tenderloin before she left on her week off. Smells good, doesn't it? I'm simply adding the finishing touches."

Sierra chuckled. "Who twisted her arm to take time off? I didn't think she'd ever left the farm for more than an afternoon."

Ariel answered her with a laugh. "Gavin convinced her to visit her nieces and nephews in Scotland."

"Queen of keeping the Cross men in line for all these years," Sierra lowered her voice to a whisper, "well, since Gavin's mother passed away."

Ariel nodded. "She keeps threatening to hand off the task of Gavin Cross to me."

"I believe you already have that covered," Sierra said. "He'd walk on hot coals for you."

"The feelings are mutual," Ariel replied, gushing.

Sierra grabbed a potato peeler and nodded toward several carrots lying on the counter. "I want to help."

With short, even strokes, she cut the ends off the carrots, then began shaving thin layers off the sides. Her mind wandered to Tony and their last encounter. He cared about her, of that she was certain, even though telling her was difficult. And it wasn't the SEAL thing. He was tough as nails, but he was also human. No, his childhood or lack of one taught him pain management in a way most people wouldn't or couldn't understand.

She decided it was time to 'fess up and tell him about her past, and his baby. Their baby. A sharp stab of pain interrupted her reverie. She placed her fingers between her legs and pressed, hoping the pressure would alleviate the discomfort.

"You okay?" Ariel asked, concern plastered across her face.

"Indigestion." She fake-smiled through a second twinge of pain as she air-circled her stomach with her finger, then continued paring the carrots.

Ariel strolled across the kitchen and dragged a high bar stool to Sierra. "Sit," she commanded as she pushed the seat under her bottom.

The ebb and flow of localized pain transformed into a steady cramp but Sierra, determined not to cause her closest friend any more concern, concentrated on the vegetable preparation. Chewing the inside of her cheek helped keep her mind focused on the task at hand rather than the increasing discomfort in her belly.

"I'll be right back." Ariel patted her on the

shoulder. "You stay put."

Panic set in as Sierra's insides started to burn. "Where're you going?"

"I need to run across the yard to my garden and get some fresh parsley for the roast."

"Love parsley," she said, trying to smile. Ariel laid the back of her hand on Sierra's forehead. "You're perspiring."

Because there's a flame thrower in the pit of my stomach. "We're in a kitchen with the oven preheating. I'm fine." Sierra could tell Ariel still wasn't convinced and swatted her on the butt. "Go."

Ariel grabbed a pair of shears from the drawer and a cloth bag she kept for garden produce off the hook by the door on her way out. With her hand on the door handle, she glanced back at Sierra.

"I'll have the veggies done by the time you get back," Sierra called out as she unfolded her body in slow motion and stood, hoping the change in position would help. The door clicked shut. *But first I must relieve some pressure on my bladder.*

She didn't bother to turn on the light in the bathroom and headed straight for the commode. *Relief.* When she pulled up her panties, the crotch felt wet. *I must have leaked.* She flipped the light switch. With a quick tug, she rolled off a few pieces of toilet paper and opened the top of her underwear. "Noooooo."

A moan slipped through her lips as she dropped her head in her hands. Drops of fresh blood stained the crotch of her panties. *Oh no, this can't be happening.*

Not sure anyone could hear her, she screamed, "Ariel. I need help."

Instead of a reassuring voice, abnormal quiet for a

working farm with abundant family, friends and staff always milling around met her ears.

"Where is everybody?" She pondered aloud as she brushed damp strands of hair off her face. "Damn, it's hot in here." She eyed the cold-water tap and thought how good cool water would feel splashed on her face.

Braced against the counter next to the commode, she pushed up and steadied herself while she raised her pants around her waist. Her hands trembled, and her knees wobbled but she managed to turn on the faucet and splashed two full palms of water on her face. After patting dry with a towel, she realized she couldn't wait for assistance or even lie down. She had to find Ariel.

The twisting in her gut intensified, taking her breath away. She bent over, clutching her belly and breathing fast and shallow. Stabbing pain, so excruciating, immobilized her. Forcing her feet to move, she inched forward, one step at a time.

The jangle of keys followed by a door shutting, propelled her in the direction of the kitchen and rescue. She opened her mouth to call out, but another wave of agony choked off the words. A familiar song, the one Ariel always whistled when she was happy, floated down the hall. Sierra closed her eyes against the mind-numbing stabbing in her lower belly.

"Thank God," she wailed and stumbled toward the comforting sound.

"Sierra, my God. What's wrong?"

Relief, hope and silly joy flooded her senses as well-defined arms offered the support her own wobbly knees refused. The room spun. "Help me."

****

She didn't know how long she'd been out, but

Sierra found herself curled up in the back seat of a four-door truck speeding down a road with Ariel kneeling on the floorboard by her side, two forefingers pressed against the inside of her wrist.

"Who's driving?" she spoke the first thought she had. And before Ariel could answer, she asked, "Where are we going?"

"Gavin is driving, and we're headed to Munroe Regional Medical Center," Ariel replied.

Sierra's throat constricted against the massive fear in her heart. "Am I losing the baby?"

From the driver's seat, Gavin said, "Not if we can help it."

Sierra strained to push herself up on one elbow, eager for a view of their proximity to the hospital and medical help for her baby. A massive wave of nausea curled her back into a ball. "What's my pulse?" she asked, desperate for information.

"Try to stay calm." Ariel placed the rubber tips of a stethoscope into her ears and positioned the cold plastic disc on Sierra's chest. "Deep breath for me."

"Geez. Warm that thing up, first." Sierra snapped as the cold connected with warm skin and immediately regretting her bitchy tone. "Sorry."

"Shush." Ariel smiled, put her finger over her lips and then continued listening. When she finished, she stated, "breathing's normal, lungs sound clear."

Sierra grabbed the corner of the paper and viewed the number. "One hundred! My pulse is normally sixty." She clutched her chest as it tightened. *Full panic mode, coming right up.* "Why is it so high? What does the number mean?"

"It's a little high but still within normal range,"

Ariel said in a calm tone as she patted her friend on the leg. "ETA, Gav?"

"Fifteen minutes. We're about halfway there." The glow of headlights whizzed by on the right. Sierra could tell by the sounds of the car on smooth pavement they were on the interstate.

Closer to help but would it be in time? Faith. I need faith. Ariel, who always functioned with extreme confidence under stress, fumbled her cell phone out of her pocket. It flip-flopped in the air; Ariel caught it before it hit the floor.

"You okay?" Sierra whispered.

Ariel nodded, her hands visibly shaking as she forced her fingers to punch in numbers. "Emergency room, please."

Endless seconds passed before someone, Sierra assumed an intake nurse, answered. She held her breath while Ariel explained she was on her way in with an obstetrical emergency. "She's about eight to ten weeks along with severe abdominal pain."

After relaying the vitals, there was a several second pause. *What the heck is the nurse saying?* Ariel's face contorted but she grabbed and held Sierra's hand before continuing, "Yes, she's bleeding."

"Put her on speaker phone," Sierra yelled.

"Other symptoms?" Ariel repeated the question, and relayed the nausea and dizziness. "Pain level?"

Sierra responded by raising nine trembling fingers. She couldn't be brave any longer. Nor could she stem the flow of grief building up in her chest. Choked by fear, she started to weep. She swiped away tears as they dripped down her neck.

Ariel commanded, "Gavin, step on it."

"Final stretch. We'll be there in five."

A street sign whipped by, but Sierra read the letters, 1st street, and realized they were almost there. *God, please save my baby.* She rubbed deliberate, circular affirmations on her belly.

As if Ariel read her mind, she said, "They'll do everything they can to save the baby."

Gavin braked hard as door from the E.R loading dock swung open. Within seconds, two people in scrubs approached, one dispatched a litany of orders while they lifted her from the car seat onto a gurney. She reached her hand out for Ariel, but a firm hand pressed her shoulder back onto the bed.

The next thing she knew was the tube from an IV swinging languidly overhead. *When did that happen,* she wondered. *I don't remember anyone inserting the needle in my arm.* Dull green walls whizzed by in a blur. Voices buzzed. A crowd of masked faces surrounded her.

She wanted a familiar face, an undeniably handsome face with deep dimples and a boyish smile. She wanted Tony.

Chapter Twenty-Eight

Tony Franco, misfit.

His grandparents used the tag to justify dismissing him from their lives. He fought hard to overcome the stigma by attending college, joining the Navy and completing the grueling training required to serve on the SEAL Teams. With aspirations of a medical career after the military, he completed the disciplined qualifications to become a corpsman, but his father's family still didn't accept him as one of their own.

He glanced in the rear view mirror as the dust from the Chesterfield County Fairgrounds swirled in an exit trail behind Candi's bright red car. There would be enough shame, blame and regret to go around later but right now he was hell-bent on doing the right thing, his interpretation of the right thing anyway. Which meant checking on Candi who'd been taken to a hospital about twenty minutes from the fairgrounds. She was his charge and his responsibility. Once he set her straight on his feelings for Sierra and the fact there was not a maybe in his mind, she could find someone else. Her injuries would heal, and she'd move on.

Tony's phone buzzed. He glanced at the vibrating screen. *Gavin. Not in the mood to catch your load of crap, dude.* He tapped end call. Speaking aloud to the phone screen, he said, "I'll call you back, bro, after I've checked on Candi and I'm halfway to your farm and it's too late for you to convince me I'm wrong."

With his phone GPS guiding him, Tony zipped along the back roads, a weight lifted by the mere fact he had chosen his own course and could give a rat's ass whether anyone labeled him a rule breaker. The ghosts who haunted him most of his life and had driven many of his decisions in his desire for acceptance, were vanquished. He opened the driver's side window and stuck his elbow on the ledge. The air whipped through his hair as he tapped the steering wheel in rhythm to the heavy drum beat of a rock song.

Weeks of trying to normalize an impossibly abnormal situation had taken their toll. Today, right now, the knotted muscles in his back eased and his shoulders relaxed. He could handle the known obstacles such as assassins taking their best shot at collecting a bounty, and Sierra's pregnancy with his child. What hampered him the most was the internal barrier of his own indecision.

His thoughts drifted to Sierra. There would be things to work out like where they'd live, how soon, but not if, they got married. His son or daughter would have a last name; his. Then he wondered, *what kind of father will I be? Better than mine for sure.*

His phone vibrated. *Gavin again.* "Jesus, Dude. Give it a rest." He tossed the phone in the back seat. "Whatever it is can wait."

****

Tony ducked his head in the door of hospital room and verified the occupant. "Candi Cane." He smiled. "How you feelin'?"

"Dumb question, Tony," she said, sending him a 'you're as dumb as your question' look. Her brow relaxed as she winked. "But I am happy to see you."

"I talked to the doctor. Seems like you'll live, you little dare devil." He moved around the bed to her head and teased her with a light thump on her forehead. "I see you had a slight concussion. Good thing you have a hard head."

Candi laughed and grabbed her sore ribs. "Ouch. Don't make me laugh. It hurts."

"Okay, but on a more serious note…." He propped himself on the edge of the bed. "We need to talk."

"Wait," she interrupted, "I know what you're going to say and it's okay. While it's true I had a mad crush on you—a mad, crazy crush—I know your heart belongs to someone else." She inhaled a jerky breath and then exhaled as she spoke. "Sierra."

"Sierra." Tony said in the same moment and then smiled. "We seem to agree on something."

"It wasn't too hard to figure out once I observed you two together," she said. "I hope this won't affect our working relationship."

Tony adopted his best poker face. It wasn't possible to let Candi know everything, but he wanted to tell as much of the truth as he could. "Of course not. The show must go on and it wouldn't be the best show without you." It was misdirection, but she bought it.

"So, we're good?"

"We're good," he answered, then after a thoughtful pause, joked, "as long as you don't mind me using your car while you're in here."

"Of course not, silly," she said, waving him off.

"Thanks. Time for you to get some rest." He stood and tucked the sheets at the base of her neck. With a wink and a thumb's up, he left the room and strode into the hallway. Peering both ways, he spotted an exit sign above a door at the end. Walking with a casual gait, he reached the entryway, and through the square window, observed several descending floors of stairs. *Empty.* He jogged down the three flights straight into the emergency room entrance. *Perfect!*

He chuckled at the irony and exited out the single side access. Except for a police car and an unattended ambulance, the driveway was vacant. Tony hustled to Candi's car and sped out of the parking lot, switching his focus between his rear view and windshield until he was certain no one was following him. *All clear.*

****

With one barrier to his exit from the circus out of the way, Tony planned to tackle the more challenging task of repairing his altercation with Alex.

Worst case scenario, he'd commute until Sierra delivered the baby, so the old man wouldn't be left in a lurch. There was still the matter of terrorists searching for him but if they had found the schedule like Gavin thought they did, he'd be better off at Gavin's farm and away from the circus. These guys were after his head, and they wouldn't hesitate to eliminate anyone who stood in their way.

As he pulled into the field dubbed the staff parking lot, he noticed a crowd of circus workers encircled around the front of his trailer. Maybe they found out he was leaving and trashed the place, he thought as he hustled toward the group. He pushed between the oversized shoes and bushy red wigs of the two identically dressed clowns he referred to as Sky and Shorty due to their disparity in size. They stood close to where Alex sat slumped over on the stairs leading into his trailer. "Hey, Alex…."

Alex raised his head and Tony gasped. "What the hell happened to you?" Tony went down on one knee and started examining the large bruise and lump on the side of Alex's head.

Before he could answer, Shorty placed an ice pack on the swollen lump. "Ouch." Alex cried out. "I was coming to talk to you about our earlier…conversation," he said, taking the ice pack away from the clown and repositioning it gingerly on his wound, "when I was jumped by these two dark-skinned males with beards." He lifted his eyebrows and Tony understood.

Sky added, "The ruckus alerted us, and we came running. They had him gagged and tied up, slapping him around but they took off when we arrived."

"You're lucky they didn't kill you, old man." Tony peeked under the ice pack and frowned. "I should have been here."

"Not your fault," Alex said, trying to stand. "I let my situational awareness slide." He dropped back onto the stairs with a grunt. "Head hurts." He sighed and shifted the ice pack.

"Take it easy. You might have a concussion," Tony said. He addressed the two clowns, "Let's move him into my trailer. We'll have more privacy and I need my medical bag."

Alex indicated with a nod of his head he agreed with the location change and waved off the crowd of workers milling around. "Everybody, please go back to work. I'm okay."

While Shorty and Sky each grabbed an elbow, Tony circled around Alex and opened the door to his trailer. Turning sideways, the clowns lifted Alex up the stairs and into the kitchen then sat him in a straight-backed chair. "Bring him a glass of water while I get my bag." Tony pointed to the cabinet over the sink before disappearing down the hall.

Alex sipped the water while Tony pulled out a penlight from his bag. He leaned in close and flashed the beam into each eye. "Umm. Pupils dilated." A bruise forming on Alex's right cheek threatened ugliness. "Hurt?" he asked as he applied gentle pressure to the area.

Alex slapped at his hand. "Hell, yes it's hurts."

"I'll bet." He removed the ice pack to examine the lump on Alex's head. "They whacked you good."

"The butt of a gun," he muttered. "Right after I refused to tell them your whereabouts."

Tony leaned back in his chair. "Thanks for that but you need to go to the hospital, my friend."

"For what?" Alex scoffed.

"An CT scan of your brain for starters."

"Not gonna happen. I have a circus to run." Alex slapped the kitchen table and winced.

"I'm advising you to go. These two could drive you while I hold down the…."

Tony studied the two clowns from head to toe. Comical was an understatement with their white-faced, furrowed brows, painted on crimson smiles and four-foot height difference. He suppressed a laugh and said, "Never mind."

"Did you get a good look at them?" Tony asked the odd twosome, changing the subject.

"Yes," Shorty and Sky both answered in unison with Alex.

"I'm going to need a description," Tony stated.

With his gaze glued on Alex, Shorty asked Tony, "Do you know what they were looking for?"

Tony glanced at Alex who nodded an affirmative on trusting these two with relaying his current dilemma. "Not what, but who. And yes…it's me."

Chapter Twenty-Nine

The steady beep, beep of a monitor crept into focus as Sierra slipped back into consciousness. Chilled air bathed her skin. She struggled to locate the covers, but a sharp yank gagged her as a man in scrubs kept saying, "Swallow, just swallow. Again, and once more swallow," then pulled a long, clear tube from her throat.

"Tony?" she asked, her voice hoarse, her throat sore. She blinked her eyes trying to focus on who stood beside her. *Where am I? What happened?*

"No, ma'am. I'm the nurse anesthetist." Sierra's body convulsed in a body shaking shiver. "Are you cold?" the man asked.

"Freezing," she croaked, "and my throat hurts."

"I'll have Frank, your recovery room nurse, fetch you a heated blanket." He signaled the man in scrubs on the opposite side of the bed, then patted her arm, and pulled his face mask off before he exited the room.

Sierra gazed around the empty space while the background noises of beeps and moans and coughs filled her ears. *Where is everyone?*

As if the nurse was clairvoyant, he reappeared and answered her thought. "I let the doctor know you're awake. He's on his way in to see you." He smiled as he cocooned her in a heated blanket.

"Ummm," she murmured. " Thank you."

"No problem," he replied as he checked the IV

line. "Your friends are in the visitors' lounge; I told them you're here in recovery."

Still disoriented and groggy she asked, "Notified them of what?"

"That the surgery was successful and you're awake and talking."

Panic hit as the clank of metal instruments, then and the acrid odors of antiseptic flashed like a thunderbolt through her mind. She snaked one hand under the blanket to palmed her stomach. Burning pain seared a path across her abdomen, "My baby."

A man wearing a surgical cap and scrubs appeared by her side. "Is my baby okay? Where's my…baby?" A sick knot in her throat choked her words as she tried to sit up.

The doctor nodded to the nurse who hustled to the head of the bed and placed a hand on each of Sierra's shoulders with enough pressure to keep her from jumping off the bed, which is exactly what she wanted to do.

"Sierra," the doctor said. "Are you familiar with an ectopic pregnancy?"

"It's a complication with the fallopian tubes."

"Correct. It's where the embryo attaches inside the fallopian tube instead of the uterus. It's sometimes referred to as a tubal pregnancy. We had to perform a salpingectomy, removal of the damaged tube."

She brought both fists to her mouth. "My baby?"

"The embryo had to be surgically removed to save your life."

"I lost the baby?"

"I'm very sorry."

Sierra tried to breathe through the sobs wracking

her chest. Tears soaked the pillow, and her body shook with the same overwhelming sadness that consumed her when she witnessed her mother being gunned down. The doctor and nurse faded in the background.

Absorbed by the grief she wondered what she'd done to deserve this, how she'd ever be whole again. A sharp click and the side rails dropped. Muscular arms wrapped around her body in a tight hug and pressed her face into a massive chest. A familiar combination of fresh alfalfa hay and sandalwood quieted her panic while a tender hand stroked her hair and whispered words of love into her ears. "Gavin and I are here and we're not leaving you."

Sierra's voice hitched. "All I've ever wanted was to be a mother."

"And you will be," Ariel crooned. "The doctor says the remaining tube appears healthy, no scarring and no reason you can't have a normal pregnancy."

My best friend, always full of hope.

A male nurse approached and said, "Let's get you in a room where you can rest." He raised the rails, flipped up the wheel stop and pushed the bed toward the exit doors. Ariel gripped Sierra's hand as she walked beside her on the right. Sierra raised her head and viewed Gavin in his typical alpha style out in front holding open the doors, waving them through.

"Do me a favor?" she asked him.

"Name it," he answered.

"Please don't tell Tony," she said as she swiped at an errant tear.

I'll grieve on my own, without him.

Chapter Thirty

Tony stood in the open doorway and stared into the empty space of the afternoon sky. In the background, the clowns continued to fuss over their boss. Sky dabbed a cold washcloth on Alex's cheek while Shorty stood on tiptoe, ice pack in hand.

The vicious attack on Alex widened the need-to-know circle. Tony opted to come clean with essential circus personnel. Otherwise, their ignorance of his situation put themselves and Alex at risk. It was anyone's guess if the scum bags would come back.

The bloodied nose, black eye and possible concussion they'd inflicted on the tough circus owner hadn't gained them any useful information, but the physical damage could have been so much worse had the clowns not interrupted their 'data gathering.' *So much worse*. He groaned at the thought, and back-stepped into the interior of the trailer, pulling the door closed behind him.

"Guys—" He signaled the clowns to sit. "We need to talk."

Sky pulled out a chair across from Tony and sat with a thud. "What's up?"

"I'm in trouble and I brought that trouble here to the the circus. The two men you tangled with are bad guys looking for me."

"Are you wanted by the police or the FBI?" Shorty

asked, giving Sky a sideways glance. "We like to keep a low profile with law enforcement."

Tony smiled at the irony. "Nothing so dire."

"Just checking. Besides, those two didn't resemble any law enforcement I've ever seen."

"Good eye," Tony replied, a hint of sarcasm in his voice. "They're ISIS hit men."

"Whoa," Sky said. "Wasn't expecting that one."

Tony gave a brief nod "Sent here by an Iraqi tribal leader who thinks I offed his son during an interrogation at a black site."

"Did you?" Shorty asked.

Tony shook his head. "I administered first aid. He was alive when I left."

"So, were you in the military?" Sky continued.

"I was a corpsman, like a medic, in the Navy." *No need for them to know I was a SEAL.*

"Why don't you call the FBI or one of the alphabet agencies and let them go after those assholes?"

"Because these guys are flying way under the radar and not on any terrorist watch list. They're assassins. We don't know their names, only that they've illegally crossed the U.S. border from Mexico. Until now, we didn't exactly know their location."

"What do you need from us?" Shorty asked.

"Let's start with a good description." With a pen poised over a yellow legal pad he'd grabbed from the counter, Tony asked, "Height, weight, and age?"

Sky blurted, "They dressed like yoga instructors." He laughed. "Except for the menacing knives."

Tony's eyes darted up. "Could you be more specific?"

"Shoulder length dark hair, almost black, long

scraggly beards and baggy clothes."

Shorty interrupted. "They were both lean, wiry, and tall, well to me they were tall."

Sky added, "Six feet, tops. One was probably closer to five feet, ten inches."

"Did they have an accent?"

The clowns exchanged a 'say what,' look. "We didn't stop to chat."

Alex said, "They spoke with a Middle Eastern accent and when talking to each other the language sounded Farsi. I'm familiar with it from my tours with the Marines."

"What were they wearing?" Tony glared at Sky and Shorty. "And please don't say yoga clothes."

"Black sweatpants and dark gray T-shirts and believe it or not, black tennis shoes," Sky replied.

"Any distinctive marking like tats? Scars?" Tony asked. "Is there any evidence of the altercation either of you might have left on them?"

"No. We scuffled a little as they shoved past us out the door, but we didn't land any blows," Shorty said.

Sky said, "We had our hands full, saving the boss."

"I need to make a phone call, but you guys did a great job. Now, stay alert. Do you have a gun?"

Both clowns nodded. He didn't need to ask Alex. "I suggest you set up a watch crew and have someone on duty twenty-four seven until we catch these guys." He opened the door to the trailer and stepped outside. Then, leaned back in. "One of you needs to take Alex to the hospital."

"No," Alex stated and pointed a finger at the clowns. "I won't leave the circus and my employees."

"Shorty, gag and handcuff him if necessary and

drag his ass to the hospital," Tony said. "And change clothes. You could cause an accident in that get up." He left before Alex could protest.

With everything going on during the last couple of days, Tony had forgotten about the calls from Gavin. He didn't know why Gavin called him, but he needed to bring him up to speed, especially regarding the assault on Alex.

As he punched in the phone number, he glanced around the circus grounds, taking in the usual sites, searching for anything unusual.

Gavin answered in a whoosh of air. "Where have you been? I've left you several messages to call me."

"Extricating myself from the circus so I can hunker down at the farm. Shit's exploding around here."

"The last time I talked to you, the rider, Candi was hospitalized with an injury. Is she okay?"

"Yeah, man but hostiles showed up here and tried to pry my whereabouts out of Alex while I was at the hospital visiting her. And now Alex is headed to the hospital from a beating and possible concussion."

"What the fuck, T-man. The situation here just got a whole lot bigger with that news."

"What do you mean?"

"Sierra's in the hospital. She told me not to tell…"

Tony cut him off. "Just tell me she's okay."

"Yes, she's okay but the…baby…didn't make it."

"What happened?"

"A fallopian tube pregnancy. If Ariel and I hadn't gotten her to the hospital…but now, anyway, we have a much bigger problem. She needs to be transported to the farm for safekeeping. If those maniacs came after Alex, they'll come after her and we can't go full metal jacket into the hospital to protect her."

Tony was already moving, breaking into a jog back toward Candi's car. "I'm on my way. I'll load up my gear and head your way. We're outside Virginia's capitol but I can be there in two days."

"You can't risk driving. Too ripe for an ambush. Fly into Gainesville. Pudge and I will come get you."

"What about Sierra and Ariel?" he asked.

"The rest of the team is in place at the farm."

"I'd feel better if you and Pudge stayed with her."

"I know but as soon as you purchase a ticket, those ass wipes will screw on their silencers. You know they're monitoring flights on the Internet." Gavin paused for a long minute before continuing. "Shit, they're probably already on their way here. If you fly, you can beat them. A case of beer says they're on the no-fly list, so they won't chance flying. They'll drive."

Tony scoffed, "What makes you think they're headed to Ocala?"

"A bad feeling, man and the fact we both know we're dealing with more than a couple of assassins. We're faced with a complex web of intelligence gatherers and hackers who are in the States, facilitating their mission. Sierra was hospitalized under her own name. They can find out where she is…or think she is. Our window is fifteen to eighteen hours tops…maybe."

"Do me a favor," Tony said through gritted teeth.

"Sure. Name it."

"Let me schwack these bastards." Deep-throated laughter assaulted his ear. Tony took his response as a thumbs-up and punched the end button.

Dread clouded his thoughts as he climbed back into the trailer, but he had to leave now. He'd accept the consequences of his actions. Inhaling a shaky breath, he put it all on the line. "Alex, I have to leave." He wasn't really asking. "Sierra's in the hospital. She's okay and I'm going to make damn sure she stays that way."

****

Tony, with Sky at the wheel of Candi's car, sped south on the interstate toward Richmond International Airport. Alex, after hearing his niece's predicament, almost threw Tony out the door. He'd even agreed to get checked out at the hospital if Tony would hustle his exit. They both concluded Sky should drive him to the airport in Candi's car and to buy time from being discovered, buy a ticket at the airport.

The only glitch was Sky didn't have time to change clothes. But what the hell. A clown in white face wearing a flame red wig in a color coordinated car, hauling balls down the interstate wouldn't attract any attention. Besides, he drives like a trained SEAL operator.

I'm good with that.

Chapter Thirty-One

"Here, take this gun just in case." Ariel offered the 9mm handgun to Sierra, butt first.

"Wasn't safety the reason you moved me to the farm?" Sierra's voice wavered as she pushed Ariel's hand away. "Wildwood Farms transformed into Wildwood Fort. All five groomsmen from the wedding armed and prowling the perimeter."

"Just a precaution. Perimeter is covered but we're talking about hundreds of acres to monitor." Ariel placed the gun on the nightstand next to the bed.

"What are we talking about? How many bad guys are there?"

"Two we think. Tony has a good description from Al...ex," Ariel started, then froze in place.

Sierra, instantly alarmed by Ariel's mention of her uncle, asked, "How does Uncle Alex know what the killers look like?" She struggled to prop herself up on her elbow while Ariel scrambled to plump pillows behind her. "Ariel?"

Ariel plopped on the guest room bed and encouraged Sierra back into a prone position. "I want you to lie back and relax, get some rest." She stroked Sierra's hair.

Sierra shook off the comforting gesture. "I'll rest after you tell me what's going on."

Ariel hesitated for a moment, then said, "They

showed up at the circus. Tony wasn't there but they found Alex."

Sierra gasped. "Oh my God."

"Your uncle is okay. And he was able to give Tony a good description of the guys who passed the information along to Gavin."

"That's a relief." Sierra screwed her face into a frown. "Tony's on the scene. What could possibly go wrong?" she said, choking back chest-heaving sobs.

"You two need to have a nice long talk and clear everything up," Ariel said.

"Yes, we do." Her neck and face flamed with anger. "I'm fed up with him not showing up. I'm giving him a new nickname: No Show Tony."

"Hey, not fair, Sierra. He cares about you and there are extenuating circumstances."

"When I consider my life before I met the charming Mr. Franco," she rolled her eyes, "I realize it was tame by comparison."

"I know this has been a rough ride, but Tony's life was borderline spectacular before some tribal war lord declared jihad on him," Ariel unfolded the blanket from the bottom of the bed and tucked it in around Sierra.

Sierra's chin began to quiver, and she wrapped her arms around herself. "I see whose side you're on."

Ariel pulled her into a warm hug. "Not at all. You're my best friend and if forced to choose, I'd choose you, hands down."

Sierra rubbed her hands up and down Ariel's back. "You know I'd never put you in a position where you had to choose."

"I know." Ariel patted Sierra's arms as she disengaged from the hug. "You've been through a lot and it's late. Get some sleep. We'll sort all this out tomorrow when Tony arrives." She stood and ambled toward the door. With her hand on the light switch she asked, "Lights on or off?"

Sierra chewed her lip. "On, please."

"I'll be back to check on you in a while." Ariel smiled and winked before closing the door.

****

Tony sidestepped as Ariel rounded the corner but muffled a grunt when she face-planted into his chest. "Didn't expect you to bolt out of the room so fast," he grunted.

Always quick on the uptake, she retorted, "Didn't expect you to arrive this soon...or eavesdrop on my conversation with Sierra."

Tony grimaced. "Unintentional, I assure you. But thanks for defending me."

She winced. "You heard what Sierra said?"

"Yep." He rubbed his neck. "No Show Tony has shown up."

"Listen. Sierra is a hormonal mess right now. Give her some time." She touched his arm. "She's not expecting you till tomorrow anyway."

"After this is over, I'll give her whatever she needs, including me out of her life." He fixed his gaze down the hall where the woman he loved slept, wrecked by his decision to pursue her. "But first I need to put an end to this goat fuck. You okay?"

Ariel slipped a 9mm from her back waistband and yanked the slide back, dropping a bullet in the chamber. "Good to go."

He stared down at her loaded weapon. "I hope it doesn't come down to you fighting my battles."

She placed the gun back in her waist band. "Correction T-Man. Our battle."

"You're starting to sound like your old man." He chuckled. "Lock yourself in your room."

She twisted the doorknob of the room next to Sierra's. "Will do."

He waited in the hall until the bolt slid shut then headed for his assigned post and the best position to smoke out these bastards: the sniper's perch.

Chapter Thirty-Two

The *pop, pop, pop* of gun fire woke Sierra from a deep, exhaustion-driven sleep. Confused and groggy from pain meds she'd taken earlier, she thought she was home and called for McTavish in a whispered voice. "Tavi, boy. Come snuggle with me."

Nothing…hummm. Maybe he got locked out of the room. She staggered to the door, flung it open and poked her head into the long, dark hallway. A shadowy form, black-clad from head to toe, seemed to float down the far end of the hall only to stop in front of the master bedroom. *What the hell?*

She squinted in the dim light. Slender fingers appeared from the flowing shroud and jiggled the doorknob. Sierra shook her head. *I must be dreaming.*

The figure, tall and slim, shoved one shoulder against the wood door, causing it to creak on its hinges. At the same time loud gun fire erupted, accompanied by muffled screams.

Sierra snapped fully alert and shrieked, "No, not dreaming!"

The figure swiveled. Sierra caught the glint of a knife sliding from the folds of the gown. Fear sucked the air out of her lungs and constricted her throat where a scream hung. *The woman in the pet store…same…dead…eyes. Oh God.* She froze.

With the knife clutched in a raised grip, the woman

charged like a single-minded zombie desperate for fresh meat. *Move or die.*

Sierra grabbed a lamp from a narrow table and heaved it at the attacker. Not waiting around to verify the accuracy of her aim, she scrambled back into the room, and whirled to slam the door. As the lock clicked into place, an accented scream of, "You bitch," penetrated the barrier. The wood frame of the door smashed into Sierra's face, propelling her backwards.

Stunned, she grappled for anything to use as a weapon, but tripped on the edge of the area rug and sprawled backward on the floor. A knee slammed into her sore stomach and sent waves of nausea straight up her throat. The cold, sharp edge of a blade pressed into her neck. Warm iron-tainted liquid trickled down her neck. *I'm NOT going to die.*

With her attention riveted on survival, Sierra didn't notice Ariel bolt into the room until she gripped the assailant in a head lock, placed the muzzle of her weapon on the woman's temple. "Drop the knife or I'll pull the trigger."

The knife hit the ground with a thud. Sierra thrust the attacker's knee from her stomach and rolled to the side. Ariel and the woman scuffled and in the few seconds Sierra faced away, the woman overpowered Ariel and knocked the 9mm out of her hand, sending it in an arc across the room. Sierra dove for the spinning handgun as the woman retrieved her knife and swung with wild slashes at Ariel, cutting her on the arm.

Ariel screamed in pain. She threw up her arms in a defensive posture, flinging blood on the woman's face. The attacker spun and rushed at Sierra and the gun. Hate in her eyes, vengeance on her face, she lunged, screaming, "Infidels. You killed my brother."

Sierra, with a strength she didn't think she had left, rolled to her knees and instinctively fired.

The woman staggered backward and fell. Ariel skittered sideways and stared as the body hit the floor. She kicked the knife away and raced to Sierra's side.

"My God, Sierra. You saved our lives."

****

Gavin and Tony filled the doorway, gaping at the carnage before leaning their weapons against the wall and giving each other a WTF look.

Ariel pressed her hand on her blood-soaked sleeve. "Sierra saved my life."

Gavin crossed the room in two strides, ripping off his shirt as he approached. He tied it tight around Ariel's wound. "Keep pressure on your arm." Without taking his eyes off his wife he called out, "Tony, she's going to need stitches and that's your area of expertise."

"No problem." Tony kneeled next to the corpse and using great care, peeled back the sheath. "Sierra saved all our lives." He pointed to a suicide vest loaded with four socks of C-4 explosive wrapped around the woman's chest. "Gonna need an EOD guy when you notify your FBI contact. There's enough material to blow us all to kingdom come."

"No shit. Where's the clacker?" Gavin asked, stepping in front of Ariel.

"Probably in her pocket." Tony lifted the corner of the opening and peeked inside. "Yep. Wired to her vest."

"What? An Explosives Ordinance Disposal guy is needed? Was she planning to blow us up?" Ariel asked, her voice wavering. "Can that thing still go off?" She searched Gavin's face. "And how did she get past the cameras and into our house?"

Tony perceived Ariel's escalating emotions and grabbed control of the conversation. "In all likelihood she intended it for herself and anyone nearby." He gave a knowing glance to Gavin. "In case she got captured but not to worry. It's wired so if you don't press the clacker, the electrical signal can't connect and detonate the bomb."

Gavin added, "Not sure how Jihadi Jane here got past the security, babe, but dressed in all black she'd blend into the night and with those carpet-bottomed shoe covers, she'd leave no footprints and make no sound. Standard issue for skilled bad actors." He silently mouthed to Tony, "Check the cameras."

Sierra who hadn't moved; remained stock-still on the floor, face pale, and blood staining her neck. Tony knew the signs of shock and they were written all over her face. He had to grab her attention, get her talking, crying or even screaming. Some human reaction, even if the emotion directed toward him was negative.

He thought for a second and then examined the small, round bullet hole in the forehead of the limp body sprawled on the floor "Holy crap. Great shot."

Sierra, still on her knees, shuddered and dropped the gun. It landed with a clunk and startled her. She blinked her eyes in rapid succession before her gaze focused in his direction. *Bingo*. He offered a smile hoping it conveyed his concern.

He turned his attention to Gavin. "Would you bring me my medical kit? It's in the back seat of my car."

"Sure," Gavin replied. He supported Ariel's arm as he walked her to the bed and helped her sit. "I'll be right back." He kissed her forehead before disappearing out the door.

Ariel, acting as the ice-breaker, gazed at Sierra with an encouraging smile and said, "It's over, *amiga*. You're safe."

Without waiting for an invitation, Tony duck-walked the short distance to Sierra and kneeled in front of her. He picked up the gun, still positioned next to Sierra's hand, and unloaded it before placing it on the bedside table. Then, he gripped her chin with a delicate touch and rotated her face in the opposite direction, so he could examine her neck. *Not serious. She won't need stitches.*

Her shoulders started shaking, more and more violently until choking sobs erupted from her throat. Tony sat cross-legged on the floor next to her and drew her onto his lap. He rubbed her back. "Let it all out," he cooed in a low, gentle voice.

Her arms hung loose. *She didn't reach for me, but she didn't push me away either.* He continued to massage her back to comfort her.

"The cut on your neck is shallow. You won't need stitches, only a large band aid," he whispered. She raised her head, short, sharp breaths accenting her answer. "Thanks, but Ariel needs you more than I do right now. That crazy-assed woman slashed her arm."

Gavin raced into the room carrying a medium-sized black bag and dropped it at Tony's feet. "Here you go. What else you need?"

"Thanks man. Nothing right now."

With a sweetness reserved for his wife, Gavin said, "Baby, I need to step outside for a minute or two and call my buddy at the FBI. You okay?"

"Tell them to hurry." She recoiled from the view. "A bomb needs diffusing and bodies need collecting."

Gavin snorted. "Don't touch anything. Tony, you got this, or should I ask the FBI for medical?"

"I'll get the bleeding under control before we move Ariel downstairs. Then I'll stitch her up, good as new."

After Gavin exited, Tony gently lifted Sierra off his lap and onto her feet. Then, he clambered next to her, never losing contact and guided her to the bed where she sat on the edge.

After a light kiss to her head, he scooted over to Ariel where he snapped open the medical bag and removed a few basic items he'd need to treat Ariel's wound. With a careful touch, he peeled back the now blood-soaked shirt Gavin had secured around his wife's forearm as an emergency measure.

"Hurts like a bitch," Ariel said with a wince.

"I bet it does," Tony said, nodding his head. Ariel was tough, so he gave it to her straight. "You're going to need stitches and as you probably suspected, antibiotics." Then he winked. "No telling where that knife's been."

Ariel chuckled at his humor. "So, are *you* going to stitch me up?" She asked with a crooked smile.

"Yes, but I'm not a plastic surgeon so there might be a scar. Or, I can do a temporary patch to stop the bleeding and Gavin can take you to the E.R. where a specialist in cosmetic surgery can be requested."

"I don't want to leave Sierra here alone."

"Understood but she won't be alone," Tony countered. "I'll be here with her."

Ariel glanced at Sierra's blank stare, then faced Tony with an urgent, *get my drift,* gaze. "Scars are sexy.

223

We can set up a sterile field in the office."

Sierra sniffled and crossed her arms. "I'll be okay by myself."

Yeah right, like that's going to happen. Like I'm ever leaving you again.

Tony rifled through his bag until he found what he was searching for; pressure bandages. He snatched two, four-inch bandages, and tore open the package of the first one. Peeling off the adhesive cover, he positioned the cotton gauze over half the wound and with a professional touch, smoothed the fabric. Glancing up at Ariel, he noticed she was focused on his procedure. He understood her interest and if it served as a distraction, so be it.

"Almost done." He tore open the second package and secured it on the other half of her cut. "You lost a lot of blood so I'm putting your arm in a sling." He smiled when she scoffed and added, "As a precaution."

Using his teeth, he ripped a piece of cheese cloth he pulled from his bag and formed half of the material into a triangle. He tied a square knot and slid the improvised sling over Ariel's head, then in slow motion, rested her arm in the opening.

"Good job, nurse." Ariel signaled with a silent nod of her head for Tony to go back to Sierra.

He shuffled the few steps back to Sierra, his medical bag in tow. "Let's have a closer peek at the cut on your neck." He smiled when she nodded approval. *God she was beautiful, and he sucked for involving her in this cluster fuck.*

Without taking his eyes off her face, he brushed aside the dark curls covering her neck and the surface wound. Her scent of honeysuckle and vanilla tantalized him. Tearing his gaze away from her soft, tell-all eyes that mirrored every emotion in her heart, he realized his work was cut out for him.

The best things in life weren't easy and as his Master Chief in the Teams often harped and, he reminded himself, he'd brought this on himself. One thing was for sure. He'd do whatever it took to get the two of them back on track. The large antibiotic-filled band-aid aligned perfectly over the three-inch cut and her golden-brown skin.

He lifted her chin and asked, "All better?"

Before she could respond, Gavin returned and relayed the conversation he'd had with his contact at the Bureau. His friend in the FBI, along with an explosive ordinance specialist, were both on their way. They'd remove the bodies and file the paperwork and with any luck, misdirect the media. "I told him we didn't need a medic, T-man."

"You'd be correct," Tony replied. "Stab wounds are my specialty." He winked at Ariel and asked, "You have antibiotics on the premises?"

"Of course."

"Ones humans can take?"

"Silly man. They're the same only smaller dosages."

"Start taking them, please. Gavin, why don't you take Ariel downstairs. She can give you instructions on setting up a sterile field. I'll be down in a few minutes to sew her up."

Gavin nodded and helped his wife stand, careful not to jar her sling. With a gentle kiss on her lips, which she eagerly returned, he wrapped one arm around her waist and steered her toward the door. As they exited down the hall, Ariel laughed and said, "I can walk. It's just a cut on my arm."

Silence hung like a heavy curtain in the room. "Want something to drink?" Tony asked, kneeling next to Sierra. Feeling like a pimple-faced high school boy at his first prom he continued, "Like a glass of water?" *I'm such an idiot.*

She didn't respond but continued to stare at the dead body with a dazed expression. Aware he was stepping into an emotional minefield but unwilling to let her suffer one more second, he lifted her into his arms and carried her from the nightmare. Down the stairs and out the back door of the house to the patio and pool area, he strode; a man on a mission. He wanted to get her back to the beginning. She started to cry, softly at first but as they traveled farther from the house the sobs exploded into gut-wrenching wails.

"Let it out, baby. Lean on me. I'm here and I'm not going anywhere."

Sierra lifted her head from his chest and raised her tear-filled eyes. "I lost the baby, our baby." The words spilled out as she choked back more sobs.

His heart squeezed until he couldn't breathe. Grief choked in his throat. "We can have another one—or an entire soccer team." He murmured into her hair, hiding a smile, embracing hope. "Whatever you want."

She inhaled a shaky breath and looked at him through tear-filled eyes. "You'd want a soccer team?"

"With you, I do." He squeezed her to him and breathed in the exquisite smell of promise, of belonging and family.

She exhaled long and slow. "I killed someone."

With a gentle motion, he laid her on the chaise

lounge and knelt beside her, gripping her hands and holding them to his heart. "You did...thank God or she would have killed you and Ariel and possibly all of us."

"The FARC trained me to be a fighter without conscience, a killer." She yanked her hands from his. "Only luck prevented me from fulfilling that destiny." She shuttered as her voice trailed off. "Until now." A shiver coursed through her petite frame, followed by another and another.

Tony shook off his jacket and placed it around her shoulders. "Sierra, you're the bravest person I know, and I've served with some damn fine warriors. I can also recognize a stone-cold killer. Sorry to disappoint you, sweetheart, but the one thing they lack, you have in spades."

He paused while she examined his face, her eyes big and round in anticipation of his answer.

"Remorse," he said. "Bad men or women relish the idea of inflicting pain. Somewhere in their twisted minds, you deserve what they unleash on you."

"Thanks Tony. You always know what to say and I believe you. I put the dark part of my life behind me. I always appreciated the safety of living in this country...until the whole assassins at large thing." She shook her head. "The paralyzing fear of knowing the threat was there but not knowing where or when I'd see you again, if ever, almost debilitated me."

He swallowed hard. "Please, forgive me."

"Forgive you for what?"

"For putting you in danger. I was warned, but I pursued you anyway. Then, when the threat arrived, I disappeared. I wasn't here when you needed me the most. I didn't protect you."

"You're a horrible person, Tony Franco."

He hung his head and nodded, too riddled with fear and guilt to face the dismissal, he was certain would come next. But a finger lifted his chin and he found himself nose to nose with the one woman he wanted by his side forever.

"Just get it over with." His chest clenched so tight he could barely breathe. For a moment he replayed the smirk on his paternal grandfather's face when the indifferent asshole lifted Tony's chin and referred to him as a bastard child before turning his back and walking out of his young life.

"I'm not going to forgive you." He swayed from the hammer of emotion that slammed into him.

She continued, "Because there's nothing to forgive. You didn't cause me to lose the baby. Neither are you responsible for some crazy warlord deciding to make you the target of his revenge."

Tony shook his head in disbelief. "I, I pursued you and put you in danger."

"Why did you?"

He stuttered and then spit out the hardest three words he'd ever said. "I love you."

She hesitated before answering. "I…." Suddenly a pulsing whump, whump, whump jerked her attention skyward. "What's that noise?"

Tony's eyes followed the sound as it drew nearer. "It's a helicopter. Probably the FBI." He was desperate for Sierra to finish her thought. Did she love him? Or, was it, I don't want to ever see you again, but she was already standing up, her attention glued to the helicopter which had now come into view? He'd have to wait.

Chapter Thirty-Three

Ground trash swirled around them as the helicopter hovered above the tree line. A bright beam spread over the property as the copter started its pre-dawn descent in the field behind the pool area.

"We'd better go inside," Tony said, wrapping his jacket around Sierra's shoulders. Glancing back at the rush of people climbing off the bird, he steered her toward the kitchen entrance where he surmised his teammates would all be assembled and ready for the onslaught of questions. There was also the matter of Ariel's stitches.

As soon as they entered the house, Ariel pulled Sierra next to her at the counter sink, handed her a glass of water and a smile. The six guys all filed in and took seats at the kitchen table. Only Gavin remained standing, peering out of the screen door. Tony drummed his fingers on the table and viewed the rest of the group. *Casual like they'd just enjoyed a day at the beach.* He stilled his fingers and glanced at his handiwork on Ariel's arm.

Gavin swung open the door. "Frank." He stuck out his hand. "Thanks for coming."

Frank, Gavin's FBI contact, dressed in a black T-shirt, and a pair of alligator boots sticking out from straight-legged jeans, didn't fit the stereotype of an FBI agent. Older than Gavin with an easy smile and longer hair than the usual buzz cut, he came across as a man who didn't easily conform to the rules; lucky for them.

"No problem. I take it we have a crime scene?" he asked, cool as a cucumber. "Body count?"

"Four males outside, female upstairs, all DOA."

Frank scratched his head. "I thought the intel was two Middle Eastern males?"

"One of the males turned out to be a female who was the sister of the guy killed at the black site, but a jihadi all the same. She's the one wearing a suicide vest upstairs. The three additional men must have been recruited by the leader after they entered the United States." Tony responded as he stood to shake Frank's hand. "I'm the one they were after."

"I see." Frank glanced around the room until his gaze halted on Sierra. "And you are?"

Tony leaped up so fast his chair fell backward. "She's with me and has nothing to do with this."

Frank's diction became slow and distinct. "Easy cowboy. Questions are part of my job."

Sierra stepped forward and offered her hand. "I'm Sierra Sanchez, a friend of Mr. and Mrs. Cross."

Frank shook her hand and pulled out a pad and a pen. "Do you live in this area?"

"Yes, well Gainesville," she answered, observing Frank scribble on his pad. "I own a home and I work." Her words came out in a rush.

"Good to know." Frank chuckled. "No need to be defensive Miss, it is Miss Sanchez?"

"It is Miss." Using her right hand, she grabbed her left elbow as if to reassure herself and offered him a tenuous smile. "Long night."

"Indeed," he replied, then addressed Gavin. "You

mind if my team heads upstairs? I want to secure the crime scene and disarm the vest."

His warm smile irked Tony but he guessed it was meant to reassure Sierra and he didn't ask her for her contact information…yet.

After Frank leaned his head out the screen door and waved for someone to come in, he made small talk with Pudge and the other guys until a man in a blast suit complete with robot, and shield entered the house. "If you'll show our EOD guy where the body is, he and his friend, Gizmo," he flicked his thumb in the direction of the robot, "will disarm the vest."

Tony exaggerated an eye roll as he mouthed to Gavin, "Gizmo?"

Gavin smirked, then led the bomb tech out of the kitchen and pointed up the stairs to the room where the body and suicide vest were located.

The kitchen doorway provided a perfect position for Tony to keep an eye on Sierra while he observed the tech using his remote control and camera to maneuver the robot up the stairs and into the room. A few snips and the device would be disarmed. Then he'd stitch up Ariel's arm.

Tony didn't budge and neither did anyone else when Frank advised everyone to move outside to the opposite side of the house. The possibility of the device detonating now was slim and the guys all knew it.

If Frank was nonplussed by the group's lack of compliance, he didn't show it as he strolled outside and yelled instructions to his team to check for explosive devices before examining the bodies.

Had to hand it to him, the guy was thorough.

****

I know it was self-defense, but I killed a person. I took another person's life. Wonder what Mr. FBI guy will have to say about that?

Sierra's mind spun in crazy circles. Left alone in the kitchen with the guys, heads together, whispering about the recent event, she pushed the dread of possible consequences away and focused her thoughts on Tony. *He told me he loved me.* The words had impact. Their warmth penetrated to her soul and although they didn't remove the hurt, they divided it by two.

She wanted to run into the office where Tony was stitching up Ariel's arm and tell him she loved him. As she advanced toward the hall, a flash of gray darted down the stairs in front of the bomb tech, descending the stairs, holding his head gear under his arm. Tail fluffed with the hair along his back upright, the missing cat must have thought he was escaping a two-headed demon.

Sierra laughed and then called, "Tavi. Here kitty." He dashed past her without slowing down and crashed into a porcelain floor vase filled with dried flowers on his way to the pantry, his favorite hiding place. The commotion brought Ariel, Tony, Gavin and Frank charging into the room from every direction.

The bomb tech spoke first. "Fast little cat." Everyone nodded in agreement. Then he reported to Frank, "Bomb's diffused. I'm calling all safe, but someone was a helluva shot. Right between the eyes."

Sierra's knees buckled. Tony side-stepped the short distance and casually put his arm around her as a brace.

Frank surveyed the faces and asked, "Who deserves the credit for that excellent shot?" He focused his attention on Sierra. "Just curious."

Tony countered Sierra's attempt to step forward by snugging her close to his side and raised his hand. "That would be me." He exchanged a knowing glance with Gavin who with no hesitation, added his comment, "Yeah, Tony's one hell of a marksman."

With a slight smirk Frank said, "Well, per my agreement with Gavin and Naval Intelligence your names will be left out of the incident report since a few of you are in the reserves and could be called up."

"I appreciate the consideration," Gavin said and stuck out his hand. "The thought of media descending on my family's farm and the attention it would bring is more frightening than the body upstairs."

Frank returned the handshake, "Don't worry. We'll take all the credit," he retorted, with a hint of sarcasm.

Sierra appreciated Gavin's humorous attempt at diversion. Her admission of involvement, no doubt, would have complicated matters. The importance of staying incognito to these men could not be understated. She smiled at Tony. His quick thinking kept her from committing a major blunder for which she'd thank him, in very creative ways, later. Releasing herself from Tony's grip, she faced Frank with a steady gaze and said, "If we're done here, I could use some fresh air."

"Good idea. We need to finish the crime scene upstairs but you're free to go."

"We'll be out by the pool if you need anything else," Tony said, steering Sierra toward the door.

"Did you finish stitching up Ariel?" Sierra asked, glancing back at her friend.

"All good," Ariel said, patting her arm. "Gavin and I are headed to the barn to check on the horses."

"We'll help with clean up," Pudge added, then motioned to the other SEALS to follow him upstairs.

"I'll walk out with you," Frank said to Gavin.

Sierra grabbed Tony's hand and led him to the double chaise lounge by the pool seeking much needed quiet and privacy. She sat first and patted her hand on the cushion indicating Tony should join her. She started to speak but the roar of the FBI helicopter, most likely carrying Frank and the bomb tech, as it lifted off, stopped her.

The glint of early morning bounced off the metal during the turn south sending shards of sunlight streaming across the pool. With her hand shading her eyes, Sierra said, "OMG. We did an all-nighter. The sun is rising."

"Was that what you started to say?" Tony asked.

Shaking her head, she faced him. "No. I wanted to thank you for taking the proverbial bullet for me."

He scooted closer and caressed the curls off her face. "Mr. FBI would have dug into your past and I wanted to let old ghosts die with the jihadi upstairs."

"Agreed," Sierra said, then pressed her lips against his. "I love you more."

****

His heart fluttered. *The L word was what she was going to say?* The career he'd worked so hard to achieve meant nothing compared to this moment. He couldn't speak, couldn't think. She pulled his head onto her chest and he released a long, relaxed sigh, "It's not possible."

Her eyes held puzzlement. "What?"

"For you to love me more than I love you."

Sierra ran her fingers through his hair as she held

him close to her bosom. "Well I guess we have a new bounty."

He closed his eyes and reveled in the peace and the hope her touch offered him. "What would that be?"

She kissed him again, harder this time, and as their lips parted, murmured, "A bounty on forever."

A word about the author…

With close ties to the Navy SEAL community, Connie's mission as a writer is to offer the reader a realistic portrayal of men who transfer their alpha tendencies and athletic prowess into serving a noble cause.

A former English teacher and corporate executive, Connie holds a B.A. from East Carolina University. Although she spent many years in the corporate world, her first love has always been writing. She maintains a portfolio of songs, poems and stories she wrote as early as ten. When she isn't creating new plots, Connie enjoys Zumba fitness and claims her best story ideas come to her while dancing the Salsa.

Connie lives near the Gulf Coast of Florida with her German Shepherd dog and a cat who takes no prisoners.

Visit her website at:
https://www.connieyharris.com

Thank you for purchasing
this publication of The Wild Rose Press, Inc.

For questions or more information
contact us at
info@thewildrosepress.com.

The Wild Rose Press, Inc.
www.thewildrosepress.com

To visit with authors of
The Wild Rose Press, Inc.
join our yahoo loop at
http://groups.yahoo.com/group/thewildrosepress/